IN BETWEEN TIMES

Hannah Cole once lived by the edge of the Thames, like Timothy Cholsey in In Between Times, but, she says, "I never fell in, like Timothy does." She now lives in Headington, Oxford, with her husband, daughter and son.

In Between Times started out as one short story and turned into one long story in three parts, featuring three very different children – Karen, Stacey and Timothy. It was the author's first novel; her second, In at the Shallow End, and her Storybook Our Horrible Friend are also available as Walker Paperbacks. She has also written two Redwings, On the Night Watch and Kick-Off, published by Julia MacRae Books.

Hannah Cole read psychology at King's College, Cambridge and then, for five years, taught adults with learning difficulties. She later worked in a nursery school and is now a full-time writer.

Also by Hannah Cole

Hannah Cole | In between times

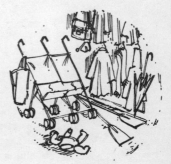

WALKER BOOKS
LONDON

For G and H

First published 1987 by Julia MacRae Books Ltd
A division of Walker Books Ltd
87 Vauxhall Walk, London SE11 5HJ

This edition published 1990

Text © 1987 Hannah Cole
Illustrations © 1987 Kate Rogers

Printed in Great Britain by
Cox and Wyman Ltd, Reading

British Library Cataloguing in Publication Data
Cole, Hannah
In between times.
I. Title
823'.914[J]   PZ7
ISBN 0-7445-1431-2

Part One | Karen

Gran was always at home when Karen got in from
school. She made Karen sit straight down to her
homework, and brought her a cup of tea. If Karen had
spellings to learn, Gran tested her. Then she gave
Karen jobs to do.

"I don't mind the work," said Gran. "In fact I can
do it a good deal faster on my own. But I would never
forgive myself if you grew up into an idle selfish
good-for-nothing who didn't know how to iron a
shirt or wash a window."

So Karen chopped up vegetables and folded socks
into pairs and missed most of the good television
programmes. While she was working, Gran talked. It
was as though she were talking to herself. She said
anything that came into her head, and it was tiring to
listen to. She expected Karen to make interested noises
now and then. Sometimes Karen turned down the
volume on her hearing aid while Gran was not watching. She could still hear Gran's voice, but she could
think her own thoughts more easily.

But Thursday night was bingo night. On Thursday afternoon, Gran had her hair done and while she was gone, Karen had an hour to be idle and selfish. She generally did some of her homework so that Gran would not moan, and she sometimes had a pot of tea waiting for Gran when she got in. But she could watch the television and eat biscuits, if the packet was not so new or so empty that Gran would notice them missing.

One Thursday Karen came home with a plan. It had been hatching for a few days, since she had realised that more interesting things than television and biscuits could be fitted into a free hour.

First she took out her homework books and opened them on the kitchen table. Then she found the kitchen bucket and took it to her room. She hung up her school skirt and put on a track suit and trainers. She tied the laces tightly.

Karen's flat was above a greengrocer's. Next door was a supermarket. The back windows of the flat looked out over the supermarket car park, where lorries pulled in to unload. Today was early closing day and the car park was empty and quiet. Karen knew that from Dad's window you could get on to the flat roof of the supermarket. She knew because some boys had got on to the flat roof once, and had given Dad a fright by climbing up and peering in through his window.

Dad told Karen never to go on the flat roof.

"I watched them build that monstrosity," he said.

"It's made of cardboard. Put a foot on it and you'd probably end up among the baked beans."

But he had not said anything about the parapet, the little wall that ran along the edge of the flat roof. It was made of concrete and it looked quite strong.

On the other side of the supermarket there was a garden. Karen did not know whose garden it was. She could just see the top of the plum tree that grew in it, and she had been watching the plums ripen. They were ripe now. It was a shame that the ones growing on the branches leaning over the supermarket roof would be wasted. Karen was sure that no-one from the garden could reach to pick them, even with a ladder. Last week she had admired the plums enviously. That was before she had made her plan.

She opened the window, hooked the bucket over her arm and lowered herself on to the ledge below the window. It was wide enough for her feet to fit on sideways. Holding on to the window frame, she could stretch her left leg to reach the corner of the supermarket roof. It was so easy that she was surprised that the boys had not climbed all the way along and peeped into the kitchen window to frighten Gran as well.

The parapet was wide, and if any of her friends had been watching, Karen would have walked along it. But she was not going to take any risks without a good reason, so she sat astride and shuffled forwards along it. She tried to lean slightly to the right, so that if something made her fall, she would fall to the roof side and not the car park side. But she knew she would not fall.

Gradually the plum tree came closer. Karen stopped and looked at her watch. It was ten to four. She would allow herself fifteen minutes for picking plums, another fifteen to get back along the parapet, and that would leave five or ten minutes to hide the plums, put the bucket back in place, and sit down looking as though she had been thinking about homework.

Sitting up on the wall she was surrounded by the branches of the plum tree. There was a soft wind rustling the leaves. The people whose garden the tree grew in could hardly have seen her if they had been standing at the foot of it. Karen began to fill her bucket. The plums had a pale bloom which rubbed off where she touched them. They were just right, not quite soft, and glowing a pinkish gold.

Karen did not stop to eat any of the plums. She wanted a good store of them. She meant to hide them at the back of her cardigan drawer so that she could eat them whenever she felt like it. She went on picking until the bucket was three-quarters full. She hardly had to move, the plums were growing so thickly on the tangled branches. That would be full enough. The bucket might swing a little on the journey back, and she did not want any to spill.

It was a shame to leave so many plums behind. It was only four o'clock. There would have been time to fill two buckets. There was certainly plenty of time to get back to the flat before Gran got in from the hairdresser's. Karen fitted a few plums into her pocket, then turned round on the parapet to face the other way, holding on to the branches of the plum tree.

Setting off again towards home, Karen thought the wall seemed a little higher than before. The bucket was heavy and the handle cut into her arm, so she unhooked it and put it on the parapet in front of her. Each time she shifted herself forwards, she pushed the bucket on ahead of her. She went slowly, whistling quietly through her teeth, and keeping her eyes on the bucket so as not to think of the drop below.

Something made her look up. There was something different about the outside of their flat. Two of the windows were open, instead of one: Dad's bedroom, where she had climbed out, and the kitchen. Karen shut her eyes. If the kitchen window was open, Gran was home. Karen felt that if she opened her eyes the sight of Gran looking out at her might make her lose her balance.

Gran spoke very quietly, so as not to startle Karen, but Karen felt that every word was knocking her off balance.

"Open your eyes this very minute, you wretched child!" whispered Gran. "Get down off that wall!"

Karen kept her eyes shut and said nothing. She leant a little to her left, the side of the flat roof. She thought she would rather fall through onto a stack of baked beans than go back to face Gran in the flat. She reached up and turned the volume on her hearing-aid right down. She could still hear Gran, but Gran wouldn't be sure that she could.

"Don't be so insolent!" hissed Gran. "Open your eyes and turn that thing on! I'm not having you ignoring me like that! I know you can get down if you want to. And you'd better, or I can tell you there'll be trouble."

"I'm not getting down," said Karen. "You'll smack me if I do. I'm staying here."

She opened her eyes. Gran's neatly curled head, fresh from the hairdresser, was leaning out of the kitchen window.

"I won't smack you," said Gran, but her fists were clenched on the window-sill. "Just come back in, and I'll not lay a hand on you. How did you get up there? Along that parapet? Come along this minute, Karen."

"Do you promise you won't hit me?" asked Karen.

"Of course I promise," said Gran impatiently. "Just come back in and you can have whatever you like best for tea."

That sounded unlikely, but Karen noticed that she was hungry.

"I'll have fried chicken, please, Gran," she said, "and rice with things in it, and we can make these into plum crumble for afters."

Gran leaned back and took a deep breath. "I'll crumble you and your plums!" she shouted. She had forgotten to be careful about startling Karen. "It will be bread and water for you for a week when I get you back on dry land. You'd better come back quickly or I'll give you fried chicken!"

"You are going to smack me!" screamed Karen. "I'm not coming down."

"You get down this minute," said Gran. Her voice was getting higher and the words came out faster. "What will your father say when he gets in and finds you half a mile above the ground? He's told you about that roof. You're not safe to be left alone. If I was any younger I'd come out there after you and let you know what I think of this. I'll kill you if you break your neck falling off that ledge. I'm going to make myself a cup of tea, and if you're not back in here by the time the kettle's boiled, I'll . . ."

Gran's head disappeared and the window closed firmly. A little later Karen saw her face against the glass. Mrs Appleton from the shop downstairs was with her. She must have come up to help Gran worry.

I'm not going back while Gran's in that mood, thought Karen. I'll stay up here till Dad's home.

She wriggled to stop her legs going to sleep. The wind was getting stronger and it was cold. Her stomach rumbled. She ate a plum.

Karen | CHAPTER TWO

Karen lay in bed. It was late, and Gran had turned the television off. Karen had been sick three times, and the kitchen bucket was next to the bed in case she was sick again. Her throat was sore, she was only just now warming up after staying out in the cold wind for hours, and she ached everywhere from sitting still for so long, but no one was feeling sorry for her. They told her she was greedy to eat the plums. Karen didn't think it was greedy to eat any food that came to hand if you were starving. Dad was late home from work and it was seven o'clock before he had leant out of the window and promised that Karen would not be punished.

Dad was horrible when he was angry, but he always kept his promises. Once he had promised, Karen started to shuffle back along the parapet. Then Gran stopped being anxious about Karen and got angry about the bucket that Karen had taken without permission. Dad took the bucket in through the window and then lifted Karen in. Karen's legs folded up under her, and Dad just left her sitting on the floor. Karen thought it was not fatherly of him. That was when she was sick for the first time.

Gran was worried about the stolen plums that they could not give back because Karen had eaten them. She went straight round to the house with the plum tree and took with her all the plums that were left except the ones that had got squashed in Karen's pocket. She would have made Karen go with her to apologise if she had not been sick. But no-one was living in the house. That was why the plums had not been picked.

"I suppose we can keep these few plums," said Gran. "They would only have gone to waste on the tree. But that child is not having a single one of them. I'm blessed if I'm ever making her another of her plum crumbles."

Karen was glad that she would not be having any of the plums. She had had enough for a while. She lay aching in bed and listened to Gran telling Dad yet again how she had felt when she came home early from the hairdresser's and saw Karen sitting on the parapet. It turned out that Karen had been very cruel in giving Gran such a fright, because it was bad for her blood pressure and she probably would not sleep a wink all night. Karen thought that was unfair because she had specially planned it so that Gran would not be worried. It was not her fault that Gran had come home early.

Now that the television was off, Karen could hear

every word from the living room. Sometimes Dad was agreeing with Gran that Karen was a greedy, thieving, selfish hooligan who had climbed along the parapet just to upset Gran. Sometimes he was telling Gran that Karen was only a little kid, and he had nicked a few plums himself when he was a lad, and it was quite a wide parapet really. Gran was not listening to what Dad was saying, and the conversation seemed to be going round in circles. Karen's eyes closed, but she woke again with a start at the sound of something new.

"You couldn't, Alan!" she heard Gran say. "I've never been one for farming out children. Folks should take care of their own. She's not a bad child. Perhaps she hasn't been having all the discipline she needs. I dare say it's my fault as much as hers. I'm maybe not all that a mother would be to her, but I do my best. Just get locks put on those windows."

Karen listened in horror. 'Farming out children' sounded terrible. She wondered what a child farm could be. Perhaps Dad was talking of sending her to boarding school?

"No, Mum, I've been thinking about it for a while," Dad was saying. "It's not fair on you to be tied down to looking after her all the time. You do enough for us, with all the housework. It's time you had a rest. And maybe Karen would enjoy a bit more of the company of other children. It might keep her out of mischief."

Karen's eyes felt hot and suddenly tears began to

slide across her nose and into her ear. She rolled over and took a big bite of the pillow so that Gran and Dad would not hear her crying. She was so worn out that she fell asleep crying and dreamed about farmers picking children off trees and putting them into huge buckets.

When she was asleep, Gran came in and straightened her blankets.

I suppose I wasn't perfect myself, she thought. I remember the beating I had after I climbed up the lamp-post and stuck Pa's hat on the top of it.

She went back to the kitchen and thoughtfully ate a few of the stolen plums. They were good.

Karen | CHAPTER THREE

When Gran's alarm clock went off, Karen pushed back her blankets and slid off the bed into her slippers as usual. Her arms and legs felt heavy. She remembered, as though she were remembering something about a stranger, that Dad was going to send her away to live somewhere else. It no longer shocked her. She was resigned to it.

Karen wondered how Gran would behave this morning. It was Gran's rule that once Karen had been punished for some piece of mischief, the business was not mentioned again. But yesterday's trouble had not ended in a punishment, unless being sick three times counted as punishment, and Karen was not sure whether Gran would still be complaining about the plums, the parapet, and her blood pressure.

"You awake yet, you scalliwag?" Gran called. She must have decided to forget about yesterday. She sounded very cheerful. She was probably happy at the thought of getting rid of Karen.

"Yes, Gran," said Karen, and pulled off her

pyjamas. "I'm up."

She wondered whether Gran and Dad would tell her at breakfast about their decision. Perhaps they would wait until they had chosen which boarding school to send her to. They would probably try to be specially nice to her while she was still with them. Perhaps it was still worth one last try at being specially nice to them, to make them change their minds. But Dad had sounded as though his mind was made up, and Karen felt that she had quite forgotten how to be nice to anyone. She combed her hair and went through to the bathroom.

"You look full of the joys of spring this morning," said Gran.

"Morning, Gran," said Karen.

Gran had boiled some eggs for breakfast, which was not quite unusual enough to count as a special treat. Karen wished she hadn't, because she hated washing up the egg spoons afterwards. The yolk was like superglue. She ate her egg carefully so that none of the yolk trickled down the side of the egg-cup.

"You had better have some toast," said Gran. "Settle your stomach." It was the only time she mentioned what had happened yesterday.

Karen ate the toast and drank the tea. Dad stumbled into the bathroom to shave. When he came out, Karen was washing the dishes.

"She's a good girl most of the time," he said. "Isn't she, Mum?"

"She never remembers the bottoms of the plates,"

grumbled Gran. "Covered in butter and crumbs, sometimes, after she's finished with them."

Dad sat down. Karen washed slowly, to give him a chance to break the news to her. She was already feeling calm and dignified. It would have been useful to burst into tears. Dad might have changed his mind then. But Karen could never cry when she wanted to, so she decided to be dignified instead.

Dad banged his egg with the spoon and began slowly to peel the shell off. He put each scrap neatly down on one side of his plate.

"Karen," he said, and drank a mouthful of tea.

"Yes, Dad," said Karen, and scraped some egg off Gran's plate with her finger-nail.

"No more climbing out of windows, eh? You did give your gran a fright, you know."

"All right, Dad," said Karen, and piled the plates on the rack.

Dad spread marge on his toast. Usually he put a blob in the middle and squashed it down, but today he made it go right out to each corner. Karen watched him as she dried the cutlery. Gran got up and went to her room. "Coward," thought Karen.

"You know Mrs Cumnor who works with me?" said Dad.

Karen was surprised. Perhaps Dad was going to lend her to Mrs Cumnor. That would not be too bad. Mrs Cumnor had some children of her own and when they were naughty she just laughed at them and shrugged her shoulders. Karen liked her.

"Yes, of course I know her," she said. "She took me to the pantomime last year, didn't she?"

"Well," said Dad. "She has to start work at half eight, the same as me, and she doesn't finish till half five. Before school and after school her kids go to a child-minder. It's a woman who looks after a few children whose parents are working. I've been thinking of looking out for one who would take you on."

Dad buttered another slice of toast. He never had more than one. He looked up at Karen from under his eyebrows and then went on spreading.

"Just before school and after school?" asked Karen. "Not all the time?"

"All the time?" said Dad. "Who would take you on all the time? No. I would drop you off on my way to work, and pick you up on the way home. You wouldn't mind, would you?"

Karen felt like juggling with the egg-cups, she was so relieved. But she sounded cautious. "Would I have to do jobs for the child-minder?" she asked. "Like housework and things?"

"I shouldn't think so," said Dad. "Just play, or watch television or something. I thought it would give Gran a break. And there might be other kids there that you would get on with. All right?"

"All right, Dad," said Karen.

Dad drew a deep breath, then stood up and put his last slice of toast in the bin.

"I'll see about it, then," he said.

Gran came out of her room. She raised her eyebrows at Dad. He nodded back.

"All settled," he said. "I'll ask Mrs Cumnor how she set about finding the child-minder for her kids. There's no rush. I want someone with a decent place. We don't want Karen cooped up in some dingy basement, even if it is only for an hour or so twice a day. All right, Karen?"

Dad looked so apologetic and embarrassed that Karen gave him a quick kiss on the arm and escaped into her bedroom to get ready for school. It was very nice indeed that Dad was not sending her to boarding school or a child farm. Going to a child-minder was so much better than what she had expected that she was almost looking forward to it. She was sure to miss some of the housework, coming home at the same time as Dad. Maybe the child-minder would have a television. Maybe there would be other children to play with.

Gran came into the bedroom. She stood by the door. Karen wondered why the grown-ups looked so uncomfortable. They had made up their minds, so they might as well just get used to the idea.

"It's not that I don't enjoy your company, you know," said Gran. "And I've done my best to do what's right. But you're getting a big girl and I'm no younger than I was, and I'm not up to some of your antics. It was your father suggested it, you know. I told him, I said, 'You can't send your own child off to a stranger to look after.' But with my blood pressure, maybe it's best. And you'll have a good time with other young ones."

"It's all right, Gran," said Karen. "I enjoy your company, too. You will still see plenty of me. I'm not going away to boarding school or something, you know."

Gran looked around for something to complain about.

"Look at you!" she said. "Haven't you ever heard of a hair-brush? What would people think? Here, give me that comb. I'll get you sorted out."

And she tugged the comb through Karen's tangles even more roughly than usual, which Karen knew was her odd way of loving her.

There was a television at the child-minder's, and for the first few weeks Karen watched it every morning and afternoon. The child-minder let her choose what programme was on, except when her son Timothy was there. He had his own favourites, but he was usually upstairs in his own room. Karen kept an eye on the clock and changed channel every five minutes to make sure that she was not missing something better on the other side.

After a while she noticed that some of the programmes were boring. She brought pieces of rope and string with her to the child-minder's and practised making knots and splices. She brought her pens and made maps of real and imaginary places. She brought the Chinese puzzle that Gran had had for years and worked at it for a whole week until it was solved. She had never had so much spare time. It was not quiet because Mrs Cholsey minded a lot of little children who cried and laughed and climbed up Karen's legs, but it was more peaceful than being at home with Gran.

"She's as good as gold, Mr Cutmill," Mrs Cholsey told Dad. "Always busy with her games. And she's quite a help with the little ones, too."

"Yes," said Dad. "She's a good girl most of the time."

"She'll be out playing on the lawn in the summer," said Mrs Cholsey. "You can only see the patio from here, but the other side of that hedge there's a bit of grass, and Mr Cholsey keeps it very nice. You'll like that, won't you, Karen?"

"Can I go out now, and have a look?" Karen asked.

"Not in this weather, dear," Mrs Cholsey said. "It's a little bit nippy and we don't want mud all over the house. Wait till the summer comes. I know you always have plenty to keep you busy indoors. It's marbles this week," she told Karen's Dad. "I think it's wonderful, the way she keeps herself amused. I mean, the little ones are not really company for her, and my Timothy is a little bit too old to join in. Marbles this week. Goodness knows what she'll be busy with next week."

Gran had got out the old marbles that were hers when she was a child. Karen brought them to Mrs Cholsey's in a bag that she had made from the pocket of her dressing gown. They were too good to have rattling about in her satchel or her coat pocket. Some were dull, dark metal, and some were plain white china, mottled with pale blue or red, but there were a few beauties. They had feathery coloured twirls in the centre, pink or yellow threads twisting one way with green or violet crossing over. Karen decided to become a serious marbles player. Mrs Cholsey let her play in the hall, where the babies could not interrupt or swallow the marbles.

"Just be sure to have them cleared away before Mr Cholsey gets in," she said. "He doesn't like to come home to a mess."

But Dad usually came for Karen before Mr Cholsey got home. Karen had only met him a few times. He looked fierce, and Karen was careful to have the marbles back in their bag before he arrived.

She was lying on the door-mat one day, taking aim with a white china at a little black marble when Timothy, Mrs Cholsey's son, came downstairs.

"Girls can't play marbles," said Timothy. "No good at shooting, either. No sense of direction."

He went on into the kitchen, fetched a handful of biscuits and went silently back upstairs. Karen had to bite her lip. She wanted to shout up, "Want a game, then?" but she knew that she was not an expert yet, and she did not want to lose Gran's marbles to someone like Timothy. She flicked the white china. It missed the black by a millimetre. From then on she practised in every spare moment.

A few days later Timothy came down, stepped over her, fetched a chunk of cake, and said scornfully, as he dropped crumbs all the way up the stairs, "You should stick to skipping."

"I can skip," said Karen. "There's nothing wrong with it – it keeps you fit. Very good for you if you're the sort of person that eats too much."

She took aim, and hit the marble square on. She was improving.

Timothy began to come downstairs more often, and he would stand in the kitchen doorway, eating biscuits and watching Karen. At first it made her uncomfortable, but then she began to feel it a challenge and it made her play better. She could use one marble to hit another and send it off in exactly the direction she wanted. She learned to control the speed of the marble, so that it stopped where she chose. She was sure that she must be as good as Timothy.

"Not bad for a girl,".he said.

"Want a game?" said Karen. She spoke casually, but she felt nervous. She could not bear to lose a single one of Gran's marbles, even one of the black ones. They had lasted so long, and she knew them all. Timothy would not love them. But she wanted to beat him.

"I don't mind," said Timothy. "If you don't mind losing some of those old things. I'll go and get mine."

He came down from his room with a net bag full of marbles. The bag had not been opened and Karen wondered what he usually played with, if these were brand new. They were ordinary shop marbles, glass with a plain coloured twist inside like a bent fish. The colours were dull: a dark orange, schoolbook green or custard yellow.

"I'm not playing for those," said Karen. "One of mine is worth twenty of yours. These are antiques."

Timothy considered. "What about if I give you an extra one of mine each time you win one?"

"The whole bag, more likely," said Karen. "No, I'm not interested. The game's off." She thought there would be no pleasure in winning, when the prize would be common marbles which Timothy could replace the next time he had some pocket money.

"Scared of losing?" jeered Timothy. "Suit yourself." He took his marbles upstairs. Karen gathered hers into the bag and went to wait for Dad in the living room. She was still a serious marbles player, but there was no point in practising all the time if there was no prospect of a match. Marbles had been banned at school since a dinner lady had tripped on one in the hall and spilled two jugs of gravy.

"Giving up the marbles, then?" asked Mrs Cholsey. She was giving the smallest baby its bottle. Karen hid behind a cushion. The baby giggled and pulled the cushion down.

"Let her have her feed, there's a good girl," said Mrs Cholsey. "I'm behind today. Michelle needs her nappy done, and the sprouts I got for Mr Cholsey's tea were poor ones. I had to chop half of them away." She thought for a while. "If you've done with marbles, how about French knitting? You can do it on a cotton reel with a bit of wool. I used to make some lovely things with it. Table mats, and egg cosies. Things like that."

Karen rolled a toy car up one of the babies' stomachs. it grabbed her ears and shouted, "More!".

When Dad came, Mrs Cholsey said to him, "Do you think that hearing aid of Karen's is strong enough? She doesn't seem to hear everything that I say to her. Sometimes she doesn't answer at all."

Dad looked strangely at Karen, but said nothing. Mrs Cholsey wondered whether he was hard of hearing as well.

Tea was not ready when they got home.

"Oh, Gran!" complained Karen. "I'm starving! I only get a biscuit at Mrs Cholsey's."

"Your gran's not a slave," said Dad. "It's not her job to wait on us. She does a lot more than her share of the chores."

"Well, she doesn't have anything else to do," said Karen. She expected Gran to snap back at her, and tell her all the unpleasant things she had done during the day: carrying heavy shopping home, cleaning the bath, or making her fingers sore darning the elbows of Karen's cardigans. But Gran was quieter than usual.

"It won't do you two any harm to work out a bit of tea," she said. "I don't want you to forget all I've taught you, Karen." She put her feet up on the sofa and closed her eyes. "There's a cauli, Alan, if you want to make cauliflower cheese." Gran was not even knitting. It was most unusual for Gran to sit down without something to do.

Dad made cheese sauce while Karen washed the cauliflower. It took a long time before she could be sure that there were no little green insects in it. She chopped up carrots and set the table and Dad made a pot of tea.

"Hard day, Mum?" Dad asked Gran when they were sitting down at the table.

Gran shook her head. "Not really," she said. "I think I'm getting old."

"Don't be silly," said Dad. "What you want is a break. Bingo tomorrow, isn't it? You'll feel fine after a night out."

He sprinkled half of the salt-cellar over his plate and began to eat. Once he started his dinner he did not like to talk, and today Karen was so hungry that she ate in silence too. When they had both finished, they noticed that Gran was not eating. She had put down her knife and fork and was leaning back in her chair.

"You all right, Gran?" Karen asked.

"Yes, yes," said Gran, rather crossly. Then she stood up. "I'm going to lie down for a few minutes."

She went to her room. Dad followed her. Karen helped herself to more cauliflower cheese and ate it quickly before the others could see that she had taken mostly cheese and very little cauliflower.

Dad came back.

"Mum's ill," he said. "I'm going downstairs to phone the doctor. Clear up the dishes so it's tidy when she comes. And do it quietly."

"What's the matter with her?" asked Karen. But

Dad had gone. Mrs Appleton in the greengrocer's shop had a telephone. Gran only used it in emergencies, or to ring up Dad's sister at Christmas. Karen thought it was the first time that Dad had ever used it.

She cleared away the plates. Usually Dad ate up any food that the others left. Gran called him a dustbin. But Karen thought that Gran might have something catching, so she scraped her uneaten meal into the bin. Then she wiped the table and began to wash the dishes.

Mrs Appleton came upstairs with Dad. She was still wearing her striped shop apron.

"Hello, Karen," she said loudly. "What's up with your poor gran?"

Mrs Appleton was always so careful to talk loudly and clearly to Karen, that it sometimes sounded as though she was talking to someone very young or rather stupid. She forgot that Karen's hearing aid made things loud enough for her anyway. She went into Gran's room with Dad and there was quiet talking. Karen dried the dishes and sat down at the table to do her homework. She hoped that Gran would be better in time to cook tomorrow's dinner. Dad had boiled the potatoes too long and they were all powdery.

When the doctor arrived, Karen let her in.

"Hello, Karen, how are you?" she said.

"It's not me that's ill," said Karen. "Gran's in there. I don't know what's up with her."

"I know you're not ill," said the doctor, "but how are you, anyway?"

"All right, I think," said Karen. She felt that a doctor would be interested in any little complaint she could think of. "I had that funny rash again, but it cleared up. And I went for another hearing test and I scored exactly the same as last time. My ears hadn't got worse at all."

"That's good," said the doctor. "And the hearing aid is still working all right, is it?"

Karen just answered "Yes," because she could see Mrs Appleton and Dad waiting impatiently at Gran's bedroom door. The doctor smiled at Karen and went through to see Gran.

After a few minutes Mrs Appleton came out.

"Well, Karen," she shouted, "I'll have to get down and see what those lads have been up to in the shop. You had better come down with me, Karen. You'll only be in the way up here."

Karen felt indignant. She had been quiet and useful. But she went down with Mrs Appleton. She liked the room at the back of the shop where Mrs Appleton stored sacks of potatoes and unripe melons. There were some very old posters which had been stuck on the shop windows years ago. Karen liked to look through them and choose which ones she would put up if she were in charge of the shop. Her favourite one showed a little girl paddling a canoe made of a giant banana.

The two boys who helped Mrs Appleton in the shop

had gone home and Mrs Appleton looked all round to see what they had done wrong. They had locked the door, but forgotten to turn round the sign in the window to say 'closed' instead of 'open'. They had swept up, but left the sweepings in the corner under the oranges. And Mrs Appleton said that there was something wrong with the till as well. It was a new electronic till and the boys were always pressing the wrong buttons. Karen thought it was not surprising that Gran and Mrs Appleton were such good friends. They both enjoyed complaining.

Mrs Appleton watered the pot plants and polished the glass shelves that they stood on. She brought out a crate of grapefruit.

"We've finished with apricots for the time being," she told Karen. She waved her hands in her own sort of sign language. "No more apricots. Can you stack these up in the rack where the apricots were?" She showed Karen how to do it. Karen always wished she could think of something very clever to say to Mrs Appleton, but Mrs Appleton always got in first with something quite silly.

Karen stacked the grapefruit up neatly. The last few had to be wedged round the side because they would not balance on the top.

"It's a good strong box," she said. "What happens to the empty boxes?"

"Rubbish," said Mrs Appleton. "No good any more."

"What a waste," said Karen. "It's a really nice box.

Couldn't you use it for something?"

"You can have it if you like," said Mrs Appleton. She forgot to speak loudly. "My Jason used to use them for all kinds of things. He had apple boxes to store all his bits and pieces in, and crates to sit on, and one summer he and his mates made a little den down on the waste land out of crates and boxes."

"I've never seen it there," said Karen.

"No," said Mrs Appleton. "That was years ago. Come bonfire night they filled it with rubbish and set a light to it. It went up really well." Suddenly she remembered about speaking clearly. "Burnt up," she said. "All gone." She waved her hands again.

"I'll have this box," said Karen. "I'll see if I can make something out of it."

They tidied the apples, and put up a 'Bargain of the day' sign on the tomatoes, which were going soggy. When Dad came downstairs the shop was ready for the morning, and Karen and Mrs Appleton were sitting in the back room having a cup of tea.

"They are taking her in to hospital," Dad told Mrs Appleton. "The doctor says she'll be all right, but she wants her kept an eye on. I'm going with her. You'd better get upstairs to bed, Karen. I'll be back as soon as I've seen her settled in."

"Don't worry, love," said Mrs Appleton. "I've got my books to see to before I go home, so I'll be down here if she needs anything."

"Thanks," said Dad. "Be good, Karen."

"You'll be good, won't you, Karen?" Mrs Appleton said, in her loud voice again. "She's been helping me, Alan."

"Bye, Dad," said Karen. "Tell Gran to hurry up and get better."

Dad went. Karen took the crate upstairs. It was not rough or splintery, as crates usually are, but smooth, with the nails neatly hammered in. It fitted into the corner next to the wardrobe and she thought that Gran would hardly notice it there. Karen hung up her school clothes and climbed into bed.

It was quiet without Dad and Gran. Karen thought of Gran in a hospital bed, and imagined her complaining to the nurses and telling the doctors how to make her better. She lay listening for Dad, but before he got home she was fast asleep.

Dad made the tea in the morning.

"When is Gran coming home?" asked Karen.

"I don't know," said Dad. "They don't seem to know what is wrong with her. She seemed comfortable enough when we got her settled in. She's by the window, so she's got a nice view over the nurses' football pitch. We'll manage all right, won't we? I'll get a bit of shopping in the lunch hour and we'll pop up and see Gran tonight."

"I'll see if I can climb into the garden with the plum tree," said Karen, "and steal some flowers for her."

"Karen," began Dad sternly.

"All right, Dad," said Karen. "Only joking."

She took a notebook to Mrs Cholsey's. Overnight she had decided what to use the grapefruit crate for: a go-cart. Before school she sat at Mrs Cholsey's table and planned how to make it. She wrote a list of the things she would need. The old push-chair was still in the shed at home and would do for wheels, if Dad had not thrown it out. Gran hated getting rid of old things, but Dad might have sent it to a jumble sale. Then there was Karen's skipping rope. She could use part of that to tie on to the front axle and steer with. She would need more wood. She hoped that Gran would let her use her tools. She was very fussy about them and always said that Dad left them blunt, or put them away in the wrong places.

Karen used the middle page of her notebook to make a get-well card for Gran. She drew Gran as a little girl, playing marbles, and wrote a cheerful message inside.

"Drawing pictures this morning, are we?" said Mrs Cholsey. She peeped over Karen's shoulder. "Don't forget to put me in it. Timothy's always scribbling, too. He's got ever so many paint boxes and sets of crayons up in his room. I suppose he'll grow out of it. His father would rather he had a more active hobby really."

Karen packed the picture away quickly. It was time to go to school anyway.

In the afternoon Mrs Cholsey came with the babies to fetch Karen and Timothy from school as usual, but Timothy said he was not coming with them.

"I'm off to the bike shop," he said. "I've got my birthday money to spend."

"Now, don't go spending it all on sweets," Mrs Cholsey told him. "Get something sensible. You need a new pump, don't you?"

Timothy ran off without answering.

"Careful of the main road!" Mrs Cholsey called after him. "Wait for the green man!"

"Do they sell sweets at the bike shop?" asked Karen.

"They only have a couple of bicycles, really," said Mrs Cholsey. "But they do repairs. Most of their trade is toys and sweets. I hope he doesn't spend all his money on jokes again. He bought some blackface soap a few weeks ago. It didn't fool anyone, and it got all over the bathroom. Come on, then, you little ones. Hold on to the buggy."

She steered the babies home and Karen followed her, wondering what Timothy would buy with his money. She had never seen him play with anything.

When he arrived home, he showed Karen what he had bought.

"Now you'll have to play me," he said. "I've got better ones than you, now."

For a moment Karen could not think what he was talking about. Her mind was full of ideas for the go-cart and she had forgotten that only yesterday she had challenged Timothy to a game of marbles.

"Let's see, then," she said. She did not think that it was possible to buy beautiful marbles any more.

Timothy took a large brown paper bag out of his brief-case.

"Come out in the hall, then," he said, "and I'll show you."

He emptied the bag on the floor. Karen studied the marbles for a while before deciding that they really were nearly as good as Gran's old ones. Timothy had bought three kinds of marbles. Some were plain glass with tiny models inside of Mickey Mouse or Donald Duck. Some were a dark silver, shining with rainbow colours like oil. Some were clear greenish glass with metallic specks of different colours.

"They are quite nice," said Karen. They were not delicate like Gran's marbles, but they were impressive. Gran's marbles were historic. These were space-age marbles.

"They cost all the money I had," said Timothy. "The shining ones are forty pence each. Ready to play?"

"I didn't bring mine today," said Karen. "I'll play you tomorrow, if you like. The Mickey Mouse ones are not as good as the others, but then my black ones are not all that special either."

"Don't forget," said Timothy. "And you had better get practising. I'm good."

Karen practised at home in the living room. It seemed a long time since she had last taken the marbles out, but it was only yesterday, and she had not lost the knack. Dad gave her a friendly game, but he was out of practice and lost all his marbles back to Karen.

"Is that old push-chair still down in the shed?" Karen asked.

"I suppose so," said Dad. "Mum never throws anything away, does she? You're a bit big for it now, you know."

"Could I use it for something?" asked Karen. "Bits of it?"

"I don't see why not," said Dad. "Nobody else wants it. I don't know what sort of shape it's in, though. When we stored all Mrs Appleton's stuff it was just bunged in on top, and the push-chair may have got a bit squashed."

Dad made Karen wash up after tea, and then it was time to visit Gran. She was still rather quiet and uncomplaining, so Karen knew that she was not well. She gave Gran the card she had made and some fruit that Mrs Appleton had sent. Karen ate most of the grapes while Dad and Gran were talking.

It was dark when they got home.

"Lend us your bike lamp, Dad," said Karen. "I'm going down to have a look at that push-chair."

Even in the faint light from the bike lamp, Karen could see that the push-chair was in a bad way. It would never be any good for pushing children in. Some of Mrs Appleton's things must have been stacked right on top of it, and the front part was crushed. The axle was bent and one of the wheels was buckled. Karen was disappointed. There was still one good pair of wheels, but she needed two pairs for her go-cart. She locked the shed and took the lamp back indoors.

"No good?" Dad asked.

"Better than nothing," said Karen. "But not good enough."

"Is it wheels you want?" asked Dad. "I'll keep an eye out on my way to work. I go past a building site, and there's always a skip full of rubbish. Someone might dump an old pram or something there."

"I wanted to get on with it right away," said Karen. "But I'll concentrate on winning my marbles tournament first, and then solve the problem of the wheels."

Mrs Cholsey brought a tray upstairs with cups of tea and biscuits for Timothy and Karen.

"Well, Karen, you are honoured," she said, as she came into Timothy's bedroom. "Timothy doesn't usually let my children into his room."

Then she noticed their faces. Timothy's was red and tear-stained. Karen's was pale and angry.

"Oh, dear," said Mrs Cholsey. "Fallen out, have you? I'm sure it's not worth it. Why don't you come down and watch something nice on the television?"

Then she noticed some broken china on the floor.

"Oh, dearie dear," she said. "Did Karen break one of your ornaments? I'm sure it was an accident, Timmy. Let's clear it away, and let bygones be bygones."

"I didn't break his ornament," said Karen. "He threw it on the floor in a temper because I wouldn't let him cheat."

"Oh, well," said Mrs Cholsey. "It's all too complicated for me. I think you'll find it's best to shake hands and be friends."

She put the cups on Timothy's cupboard and took the tray downstairs. Karen ate her biscuit, but she did not pick up her cup. Her hands were shaking and she was afraid of spilling the tea.

"My mum will make you give them back," said Timothy. "I paid for them. They are mine."

"I won them," said Karen. "You knew the rules. I risked losing my gran's antique marbles. If you had won them, I wouldn't have kicked up a fuss like that. I know what's fair."

"I spent all my birthday money on them," wailed Timothy. He was crying again.

Karen drank her tea. She was no longer in a rage. She was tired of the quarrel, and she thought that if Dad arrived while Timothy was still crying, he might make her give him back the marbles. Dad hated scenes.

"Well," she said, "if you want them back, you had better think of something to trade for them. I don't care about the stupid marbles. You can have them back if you want. But I won them fair and square and you had better admit it."

Timothy cheered up. "All right," he said. "You won them. What will you trade them for? I've got loads of games. Or a fountain pen. Or a watch. It only needs a bit of repairing."

"I've got no-one to play games with at home," said Karen. "I've got pens. I don't know whether you have anything that I really want."

"Well, what do you really want?" asked Timothy.

Karen thought for a while. "If you could find me a pair of wheels, strong ones, I would swap," she said.

"What sort of wheels?" Timothy asked. "What do you want wheels for?"

"None of your business," said Karen. "About this big. With tyres on. You haven't got any wheels, have you?"

"Wait a minute," said Timothy. "I might have."

He opened the door and ran downstairs. Karen watched out of his bedroom window and saw him dart out into the garden. From here, upstairs, she could see over the hedge to the lawn that Mrs Cholsey had told her about. Beyond the lawn were trees, and against the wall was a wooden shed. Timothy disappeared inside. He was in there a long time. Karen looked along his shelves at the books and games.

"Here you are, then," Timothy shouted, as he burst into the room again. "Let's have the marbles." He was carrying a pair of wheels, still on their axle.

"Let me have a look at them first," said Karen. "They are a bit small. I don't know if they will do." She ran them over the carpet. They ran smoothly. She thought about them for a while.

"I think they will do," she said at last. "Thank you very much. Here's your marbles." She was pleased with the deal. The marbles were nice, but not worth the fuss. The wheels were just what she needed. It was Friday, and she had brought her plimsoll bag back from school. The wheels nearly fitted into it, so it would be easy to carry them home.

Timothy began to pick up the broken china from the floor. Karen went downstairs to wait for Dad.

No-one knew when Gran would be let out of hospital. It could be any time, so Dad and Karen had to have the flat tidy and plenty of food in, ready for her.

On Saturday morning they were at the supermarket early, and when the shopping was done they spring-cleaned the flat. They took all the sheets down to the Launderette and hid Dad's beer-cans at the bottom of the bin.

"If she's going to stay in much longer," said Karen, "I wish they would tell us. Then we could be nice and sloppy until just the day before she was due home, and clear it all up at once. It's just like having her at home, having to keep everything clean all the time."

"It should make you appreciate what your gran does for us all the time," said Dad. He made a cup of tea and sat down with his feet up on the coffee table, which Gran never allowed, to watch the sport on the television.

"I'm off to the shed now," said Karen. "I'm going to do a bit of carpentry. Nothing dangerous, so you needn't worry. And I won't forget to put the tools away in the right place."

Mrs Appleton's two boys were out at the back of the shop having their tea-break. They came and watched Karen struggling to put her go-cart together. When Mrs Appleton came to call them in, they were busy inventing a steering system for the go-cart.

"Well, I'm glad that crate's being put to a good use," said Mrs Appleton. "You know how to make the brake, don't you? Our Jason used to have a piece of wood like a lever, nailed on the middle so that it would swivel. No, not like that. It has to press against the wheel when you push it down. Yes, that's better."

Karen realised that on her own she would never have managed to fix the axles onto the crate or work out the steering. There was still a lot of hammering to do, and the whole thing could do with some sand-paper, but Mrs Appleton and her two boys had done the difficult parts. Karen could not wait for her first ride.

When it began to get dark, Karen went up to the flat. Dad was asleep with the paper on his lap.

"Wake up, Dad," said Karen. "What are we having for tea?"

Dad went on snoring. Karen shook his shoulder, but he only grunted. Karen tiptoed over to the tele-vision and changed channels. Dad sat up straight away.

"I was watching that!" he said. "Put it back on!"

"Got you!" said Karen. "Now, what's for tea?"

"Anything you like," said Dad. "Leave me alone." He closed his eyes again.

"If I cook it, will you wash up?" Karen asked.

Dad began to snore again. Karen peeled some potatoes and fitted ten fish fingers in the frying pan. There was a knock at the door. It was Mrs Appleton. She peeped in and saw Dad asleep in his chair.

"Oh dear," she said. "I need to speak to your father. The hospital just rang. Hospital. On the phone. Mrs Cutmill is coming out tomorrow."

"All right," said Karen. "I'll tell him. We're all tidied up ready for her."

"You sure you've got the message?" said Mrs Appleton. "Your gran will be home tomorrow. That's Sunday. All right, dear?" She disappeared downstairs.

Karen switched off the television. Dad's eyes opened.

"What's up?" he asked. "Tea ready?"

"Gran's home," said Karen. "Sit up straight."

Dad swung his feet quickly off the table and looked round guiltily.

"It's all right." Karen laughed. "She's not really here yet. But she'll be out tomorrow. They just phoned Mrs Appleton and she came up to tell us. I expect she'll be back again in a minute. She wasn't sure if I was intelligent enough to give you the message."

Sure enough, Mrs Appleton came up while they were eating their tea.

"My," she said, looking at their plates. "You

certainly like fish fingers, don't you? Did you get the message, then? Your mum will be out tomorrow."

"All right, Mrs Appleton," said Dad. "Thanks. I'd better arrange for a taxi. What time did they say?"

"Any time after lunch," said Mrs Appleton. "You can use my phone to ring for a taxi if you like. I'll be here most of tomorrow. There's a lot to sort out in the shop. Those two boys are not a lot of help. I'll get them trained up, and then they'll be off to work somewhere else. It's always the same. I tell you what, I'll pop up later on with any of the flowers that are left. They should just last you till tomorrow."

"Just as well we cleaned up," said Karen, when Mrs Appleton had gone. "We'll polish your boot-marks off the coffee-table, and Gran will never know what you've been up to while she was away."

"I don't wear boots indoors," said Dad. "Now look, Karen, we'll have to be gentle on her when she comes home. None of your tricks and jokes. If you must fool around and get into mischief, do it at school. Try and clean up after you, and don't grumble about helping in the kitchen."

"I'll be perfect," said Karen. "Anyway, I'm going to be out of doors a lot from now on. Wait till you see what I've been making."

Gran sat in the armchair surrounded by Mrs Appleton's left-over flowers.

"I hope you cooked yourselves a proper dinner today," she said. "They do a lovely Sunday roast at the hospital. The helpings are a bit small, though, for anyone who's thinking of getting better."

"Are you better now, Gran?" Karen asked.

"I feel all right," said Gran. "I've got some medicine, and they are going to keep an eye on me. I think they wanted to keep me in a bit longer, but they needed the bed for someone else. They're shuttling people around between the beds all the time up there."

"You take it easy for a while, Mum," said Dad. "You gave us quite a fright the other night."

"Dad and I are going to do all the housework," said Karen. "You just sit down with your feet up on the coffee-table and have a rest."

Dad looked annoyed. Gran looked puzzled.

"You know I wouldn't do that, Karen," she said.

Just then there was a knock on the door. It was Mrs

Appleton. She was breathless from coming up the stairs in a hurry. Someone had telephoned for Dad.

"I am sorry," said Dad. "I can't think who it can be. There's only the school that has your phone number, or the child-minder. Unless it's the hospital, Mum. Maybe you left some of your luggage there by mistake."

"I didn't forget a thing," said Gran. "I checked the locker twice."

Dad went downstairs. When he came back his ears were red and his mouth was firmly shut

"Well," said Gran, "what was that all about?"

"I'm not sure," said Dad, "but I'm going to find out."

He marched into Karen's bedroom, and they could hear him opening and shutting cupboards and drawers. Then he came out, took the shed key down from the hook and ran downstairs.

"What's up with him?" said Karen. "Another cup of tea, Gran?"

"No, thank you, dear," said Gran.

When Dad came back, Karen could not believe her eyes. He was holding the front wheels from her go-cart that Mrs Appleton's boys had helped to fix on the day before.

"What have you done?" shouted Karen. "That's off my go-cart! It was nearly finished! Give them back! You'd better not have damaged it."

"Keep your voice down, Karen," said Dad. "I'm going to deal with this quietly. If your gran wasn't ill, you'd get a hiding. As it is, I'm just taking this pair of wheels straight back to the person that they belong to. I'll have something to say to you when I get back."

Dad closed the door quietly behind him, but they heard him stamping down the stairs.

Gran shook her head. "I hope you've not been stealing again, Karen," she said. "You are old enough to tell right from wrong."

"I've not stolen anything!" Karen exploded. "Will you just let me tell you where I got those wheels from? I know Dad won't listen when he's in one of his tempers. Will you just listen to me?"

Gran listened.

"Well," she said, when Karen had finished. "I don't like the sound of that Timothy. It looks as if they weren't his wheels to give you. Perhaps his mum or dad use them for something."

"They aren't the sort of people who make go-carts," said Karen. "I expect it's just that stupid Timothy who has changed his mind and wants them back, the same as he did with the marbles. And if he wants something, his mum would get it for him. She spoils him. But it's not fair of Dad to give in to him as well. I don't suppose Timothy will ever get round to making a proper go-cart, and mine was nearly finished. Now I'll never be able to finish it."

"Calm down," said Gran. "I'll try and explain it all to your father. If he won't see reason, I'll go over there myself and get those wheels back. It seems to me that we're owed either the wheels or the marbles."

Dad came home in a rage. He had had to be polite and apologetic to Mr and Mrs Cholsey and it had made him angrier than ever. He kept his mouth shut when he got indoors, for fear that Gran would be upset if he opened it.

"I'm not feeling very well," said Gran, "and I don't want anything to upset me. Come and sit down, dear. I want to talk to you."

Karen could see that Dad did not dare to say a word. She was longing to tell the story herself, now that Dad was being made to listen, but she left it to Gran.

"All right," said Dad. "I was wrong. I should have let you explain. But those wheels are off Mr Cholsey's golf bag. He was going to play golf this afternoon, and when he went to get his clubs, the wheels had gone off his trolley. I've never met the man before, but he's not very nice when he's angry, I can tell you. So it was that boy, was it?"

"He must have taken the wheels off while I was waiting," said Karen. "I told him I needed a pair of wheels, but I thought those were just spare ones, like the ones on our old push-chair. Well, I'm not going back there any more, with them all thinking I stole their rotten wheels."

"Of course you are going back," said Dad. "Mum's not in any fit state to keep an eye on you at the moment. You'll have to go. They'll forget all about it in a little while. And don't you worry about the wheels. I'll watch out on my way to work, and we'll pick up another pair soon enough. You hadn't put

them on right, anyway. I'll show you the prope[r]
to do it."

Karen was speechless. It was Dad who had made the
whole thing worse by not listening to her. If he had
asked her about the wheels in the first place, he could
have straightened it all out with the Cholseys, and
maybe even got the marbles back. And now he was
calmly expecting her to carry on going to Mrs Cholsey's every morning, as though nothing had happened. Karen knew she could not insist on staying at
home until school time, because she had promised to
make things easy for Gran. She could not even shout
at Dad, because it might upset Gran and make her ill
again. She felt as though she would burst.

"Come on, Karen," said Gran. "Let's go downstairs."

"What on earth for?" said Dad. "You shouldn't be
running up and down stairs. You are supposed to be
resting."

"We'll go slowly," said Gran. "Karen can help
me."

"I'm so sorry, Mrs Appleton," she said when they
got downstairs. "Do you think we could borrow your
telephone just one last time? I've brought down some
money for the calls."

"No, no," said Mrs Appleton. "I couldn't take it,
Mrs Cutmill. It hardly costs anything to phone on a
Sunday. Please do go ahead. I hope you are not poorly
again."

"Thank you," said Gran, "I'm feeling fine."

She sat down by the telephone and looked up Mrs Cholsey's number. Karen was relieved that the whole thing was going to be sorted out, but she felt like squirming with embarrassment as Gran told Mrs Cholsey what she thought of Timothy, and what she thought of Mr and Mrs Cholsey for accusing Karen without finding out the truth of the matter. Gran put the phone down and sighed with satisfaction.

"They are terribly, terribly sorry," she said. "Mrs Cholsey always thought you were such a nice little girl, and she is so sorry that Timothy didn't quite tell the truth, and he'll give you all your marbles back tomorrow."

"I'd rather have the wheels," said Karen.

"I can't work magic," said Gran. "I suppose the man likes playing golf. I can't see why, myself, but I'm afraid you'll have to settle for the marbles. I hope they're good ones."

"Not bad," said Karen. "Not as good as yours, Gran."

"Of course not," said Gran. "Only the best for me." And on the way upstairs she put her arm round Karen and gave her a rather bony hug, which was most unusual.

Part Two | Stacey

Stacey | CHAPTER ONE

When Stacey woke up, she pulled back the curtain and looked out of the window to see if the lights were on in the flat across the road. There were two blocks of flats just the same. Stacey and her mother lived in Flat 2 of the block with green doors and balconies. From her window she could see across to Flat 2 of the blue block. Stacey did not know the people who lived there, but she knew that they always turned their lights on and drew back their curtains at seven o'clock.

"Get up, Mum!" she shouted. "They have got dressed already! It must be late. Look, they are eating breakfast."

Mum came into Stacey's room in her dressing gown, and peered out of the window.

"I can't see any breakfast," she said. She had not put her glasses on yet. "One of these days they will notice you watching them, and then they will start watching you. You will hear them saying, 'Look, she is taking off her pyjamas, look, she has spilt her food.'"

"I don't watch them," said Stacey. "I just use them

to check the time. They have a cup of tea at seven and listen to the news. Then they get dressed, and then they have breakfast. At eight o'clock they have their last cup of tea and then they leave for work. It must be half past seven at least. I am starving."

She went into the kitchen to put the kettle on, and found some of yesterday's macaroni cheese still in the dish.

"This tastes better cold," she said, and sat down to eat it.

Mum shut her eyes. "What a horrible sight," she said. "I can't watch."

"You can't see without your glasses anyway," said Stacey. "Pretend I am eating bacon and egg and toast and marmalade."

"Just as bad," said Mum. "You know I hate food in the mornings. Make me some tea, will you? I am going to wash my hair."

"Whatever for?" said Stacey.

"I do wash now and then, you know," said Mum, and tucked a towel round her neck.

Stacey guessed that Mum was getting ready for an interview. Mum was always trying to get a job. Sometimes she was asked to go to a factory or a shop or a garage for an interview, and she had to dress in her best clothes and explain why she would be good at doing the job. Then the boss of the shop or garage or factory would explain to Mum that she was not quite the person they wanted for their job. She was too old or too young, or had not had the right experience or education. Sometimes they said, "We'll let you know", which meant that they didn't want her, but they were too polite to say so.

Stacey decided to be quiet and kind, because Mum was always nervous before interviews. She stirred an extra spoonful of sugar into Mum's tea, put the macaroni cheese dish in the sink to soak clean, and went and got dressed without complaining about the white socks being pink.

Mum came out of the bathroom wrapped in a towel and peered around for her tea. When she tasted it, she screwed up her face.

"This tastes like treacle," she said. "How much sugar did you put in it?"

"I thought you might need some extra energy today," said Stacey. "What job is it that you are trying for?"

"It's at the hospital," said Mum. "Cleaning the floors and taking round tea-trolleys."

"Do you know how to clean floors?" asked Stacey.

"I wash our floors, don't I?" said Mum. "What do you suppose happens to all the stuff you spill on them?"

"I have never seen you do it," said Stacey.

"I wait till you and your big feet are out of the way," said Mum. "Anyway, I don't suppose I shall get the job. There will probably be hundreds of people trying for the same job. I have to look specially clean and tidy. It is a very hygienic job. But I mustn't look too smart to do some serious cleaning."

"Wear your white blouse," said Stacey. "The brown one is nice, but you can't tell by looking at it how clean it is. I'll polish your glasses for you. What will we do to celebrate if you get the job?"

"I won't get it," said Mum. "They will probably prefer someone who has worked in a hospital before. But if they do take me on, we'll have something special for tea."

"Chips," said Stacey. "And you can get some new shoes. And can I go to judo classes?" Then she remembered something real. "Mum, I need to take some money to school for the hamster."

"What does the hamster want money for?" asked Mum, rubbing her hair dry. "It will have to wait until I have got a job. Then I'll buy a present for every hamster in the school."

"Not a present for the hamster, you idiot," said Stacey. "Poor little Smudge never came back after the last time he escaped, and Mrs Ebbs is lost without him. We are going to get a new one as a surprise for her. They cost three pounds."

Mum plugged in the hair-drier.

"Find someone who is trying to get rid of some baby ones," she said. "There is no need to get a pet-shop one. Do your hair quick before I need the brush. Have you got your recorder?"

"Recorders is on Tuesday, Mum," said Stacey. "I'm all ready."

"I'll see you after school, then," said Mum. "Be careful crossing the main road. It's not quite light yet, and the cars won't see you too clearly. And don't be cheeky to the lollipop man. I heard about yesterday. Put your coat on at play-time."

"Yes, no, yes," said Stacey. "Anything you say, Mum. Good luck with the interview, Mum." And she left Mum to get dressed in her cleanest clothes and to practise being the sort of person that hospitals like to have pushing their tea-trolleys.

Stacey | CHAPTER TWO

When Stacey got home from school, she tiptoed into the flat and decided not to tell Mum just yet about the rip in her school coat. But Mum was singing and on the table was a huge pot of flowers. Mum sometimes had a little jug of flowers to cheer herself up after an interview, but these flowers were the wrong kind for this time of year. They must have been grown in Australia, or in a hot-house. Next to them was a box of chocolates.

"Have you got another interview?" Stacey asked, puzzled. "You must be trying for a really good job if the first wage-packet is going to pay for those!"

"No more interviews," said Mum. "I've given up trying for jobs."

"What are you so cheerful about, then?" asked Stacey. "How are we going to pay for all those tiger-lilies?"

"With my first wage-packet," said Mum. "And they are not tiger-lilies. They took me on! I got the job! And I have got you some chips. Careful, don't get sauce on your school clothes."

So Mum had been for the interview in her clean white blouse and the hospital had given her the job. Stacey sat down and stared at the expensive flowers. She had never really thought about what it would be like when Mum actually got a job.

"Will we really be rich?" she asked, as she peeled the lid off the packet of sauce.

"Richer than we are now," said Mum. "We can pay off the television, and maybe get you a bike. I will have to buy one for myself right away, just a cheap old crock. I shall be starting work early in the mornings, before the buses start to run. But as soon as that is paid off, we will get a brand new bike for you. What do you fancy? Small wheels? A bike for stunts? Or a racer with ten speeds?"

Stacey stopped eating her chips. She was not thinking about bicycles.

"How early will you have to start work, Mum?" she asked.

"Seven," said Mum. "But I finish at four, so we'll have all the evening together."

Stacey felt her mouth twitching at the corners. She wanted to tell Mum that she was pleased she had got the job. But her mouth refused to feel pleased. It was twisting into all kinds of shapes, trying to get her eyes to cry as well.

"Aren't you glad?" asked Mum. "Things will be a lot easier, with a proper wage coming in. And you will have a mother with a bit more self-respect from now on. I'm a Hospital Domestic now, not just an unemployed housewife. What's up, Stace?" She put her smart ironed arms round Stacey and rubbed her chin on Stacey's head.

"I am glad," said Stacey. "I am really. It is just that it will be a bit lonely here in the mornings before I go to school. Just at first, I mean, until I get used to it."

Mum laughed. "Silly! I can't leave you here for hours on your own, can I? I have arranged everything. I have found a nice child-minder for you who looks after quite a few children. It should be fun. I will drop you round there in time for breakfast, and Mrs Cholsey will see you off to school and fetch you in the afternoon. I'll come for you when I finish work. You will know some of the other children there. I am sure you will like it."

Stacey's mouth had stopped trying to cry, and she even managed a sort of smile. But the thought of having to have breakfast each day in a strange house, and be looked after by a strange person who would probably make her drink up the tea-leaves and sit up straight at table, quite spoiled the chips.

"When do you start work, Mum?" she asked, hoping at least that it might be a month or so before she had to face Mrs Cholsey and the gang of children that she was supposed to have such fun with.

"Monday," said Mum. "The new life begins. Good riddance to the old one!"

Stacey remembered how nervous Mum had always been in the mornings before an interview, and how miserable afterwards. She tried to remind herself about the things they would be able to spend Mum's money on. But she also looked back on the friendly breakfasts before school, and the walks in the park after school. It was horrible to think of a strange person meeting her outside the school gates and taking her off to a strange house, instead of coming straight back to their comfortable flat and talking about everything that had happened during the day.

Stacey blinked her eyes firmly. "Good riddance to the old life," she said, and gave Mum a hug. She hid her face in the smart blouse that had finally got Mum a job.

On Monday morning it was misty. Stacey could see a cloud hanging round the street-light outside her window. The people in the flat opposite still had another hour or more in bed and their flat was quite dark. It was too early for Stacey to feel hungry, but Mum made her drink a cup of tea before they went out. The cold came up the stairs to meet them.

Mum got her bike out of the shed and wheeled it along on the pavement beside Stacey. A few bicycles passed them, and every squeak and click of the pedals sounded loud in the dark. Perhaps the riders were on their way to work like Mum, or perhaps they were coming home after the night shift. The postman was already working and the lights in the paper shop were on. A woman inside was sorting the papers into bundles to be delivered to houses. Most of the houses they passed still had their curtains closed.

"Nearly there," said Mum. "Mrs Cholsey lives in the next street."

Stacey had expected the child-minder to live in a

flat like theirs. The next street had no flats, only houses.

"Does she live in a house?" Stacey asked. "Will I be allowed to play upstairs? Does she have a garden?"

"I don't know," said Mum. "Here it is."

The house was square and brown with a fancy lantern over the front door. The curtains were still drawn. Stacey made sure that she was smiling as Mum rang the doorbell. She didn't want Mum to have to worry about her on the first day of her new job. The door opened. As she stepped inside, Stacey felt that she was leaving behind the old days when Mum was always around and walking into a strange new life.

Breakfast at Mrs Cholsey's was very different from breakfast at home, but Stacey decided that it was not bad enough to be worth dreading. She was allowed sugar on her cornflakes and as much toast as she could eat. When she had finished eating, she took her plate, bowl and cup to the sink to wash them, as she would at home.

"For goodness' sake, leave the things where they are," said Mrs Cholsey. "I can't stand people messing about in my kitchen." She did not say it unkindly. "If you have had enough, go and watch the television, there's a good girl."

Stacey switched the television on, but grown-ups were making stupid jokes so she switched it off again. She did a few press-ups on the nice thick carpet. When Mrs Cholsey came in, Stacey was standing on her head.

"I don't think you had better do that in here, my duck," she said. "There's all my ornaments, you see, and the fish tank. We wouldn't want them damaged. Timothy will be down in a minute. Then you can play with him. Timothy!" she shouted up the stairs. "Come down! You will have no time for breakfast if you don't hurry!"

Stacey recognized Timothy Cholsey from school. He was older than her, but Stacey thought that in some ways he behaved like a baby. He sat down at the table and waited for his mother to pour his cornflakes for him. She even sprinkled on the sugar.

"Give us a bit more, Mum!" he said, and Mrs Cholsey sprinkled on more. Stacey's mum would have said, "Do it yourself, then!"

"Don't forget my dinner money," Timothy said. "And I need my football gear today and that form you had to sign."

"It is all ready for you, dear," said Mrs Cholsey. "All packed in your bag in the hall."

Stacey wondered why Mrs Cholsey did not make Timothy pack his own bag, or get his own breakfast. Perhaps she had not noticed him growing up.

Two babies arrived before it was time to go to school. Mrs Cholsey unfolded a playpen and put the babies straight into it in their outdoor clothes. One of them started to chew the edge of the other one's coat and made it cry.

"Give him his tortoise, there's a dear," said Mrs

Cholsey to Stacey. "Just while I brush Timothy's hair."

Stacey found an old pink tortoise on the shelf and gave it to the baby. The baby bit it, shook it and threw it out of the play-pen. Then it started to cry again, so Stacey fetched the tortoise for it. It was wet with dribble and Stacey held it with one finger and thumb. She wondered if the baby spent all day throwing its tortoise away.

When the babies screamed, their faces turned red, and they looked uglier than when they were not screaming. They were both dribbly, and Stacey hoped that Mrs Cholsey would not ask her to pick them up. She shook the tortoise at the babies, but it did not stop them crying.

It was a relief when Mrs Cholsey called out, "Half past eight!" She lifted the babies out of the play-pen and strapped them into their double buggy.

"Time to go, children," she said, and hustled Stacey and Timothy out into the cold street. It was still misty, but quite light now, and the rest of the world had got up. "We have to get to school early," she explained to Stacey. "I have to be back here by nine for my other babies."

"How many babies do you look after?" asked Stacey.

"Four in the mornings," said Mrs Cholsey, "and I have two children who come here after play-school at dinner time. So you will find it is very jolly in the afternoons. Usually we have Karen here as well, and you will be able to walk to school with her and Timothy. I expect you know her. Today her father is off work, so he is looking after her. I had better walk to school with you this time, to be sure that you know the way. It will be different going from this direction."

Stacey thought she could have found her way to school by herself, but the babies were already in the buggy and Mrs Cholsey was carrying Timothy's school bag for him. Stacey did not know anyone at school called Karen. When they arrived at the school gates, she looked around to see who it might be, but there were no fathers in sight.

"Here we are, then," said Mrs Cholsey. "Have a lovely day, and I'll see you both later. Timothy likes me to meet him after school, you see, so you needn't worry about finding your way back on your own. Be good and Timothy, remember to tell Mr Witney that your chest is still not right."

But Timothy had already run ahead into the playground.

"Bye!" said Stacey, and found that life was back to normal once she was in the playground.

The mist had cleared when Stacey came out of school in the afternoon, and it had been raining. She saw Timothy come out, but he did not speak to her. He gave his bag to his mother, who was waiting at the gate with a lot of little children. She handed him a raincoat that she had brought for him. He put it on without saying a word and walked on towards their house. Mrs Cholsey hung the bag over one handle of the buggy.

"All right, my duck?" she said to Stacey. "Did you have a good day at school?"

Stacey was going to tell her about Rachel pushing her off the bench in the music class. But she realised that Mrs Cholsey had only asked so as to be polite. She was much too busy with the babies to listen to Stacey. They set off home, with the two smallest babies in the buggy, two bigger ones holding on at the sides, and two little children holding hands in front.

"Don't go too far ahead!" Mrs Cholsey shouted to them. "Wait at the corner!" The two little children stopped, and the buggy bumped into the back of their legs and knocked them over. Next, one of the babies who was holding on at the side of the buggy started to walk backwards. It had seen something it wanted to pick up.

"Come on, Alvin," said Mrs Cholsey. "You don't want that dirty stick. We'll go home and have a nice bikkie."

Alvin did want the dirty stick, and he cried when they left it behind. While Mrs Cholsey was wiping his tears away she bumped the buggy into the little children in front again. Stacey was very glad when they reached the house. She was longing for Mum to come and fetch her.

As soon as Mrs Cholsey unlocked the door, the four children who could walk went straight into the hall and stood in a row, waiting to have their boots and coats taken off. Mrs Cholsey took the two babies out of the buggy and sat them at the end of the row. Stacey slowly folded up the buggy. She thought she had better make it clear that she was one of the grown-ups and not one of the children, or Mrs Cholsey might expect her to line up and have her coat taken off as well.

She hoped that Mrs Cholsey would not ask her to take the babies' outdoor clothes off, in case she did it wrong and made them cry. By the time she had worked out the clips of the buggy and found how to fold it up, and pinched her finger, Mrs Cholsey was taking the last child out of its rain-suit and collecting up the hats and scarves. The children stood quite still in their line.

"Aren't they good?" said Mrs Cholsey. "They know they must stand still if they want their bikkie. Who wants a nice bikkie?"

"Yes please," said Stacey. "I would like a biscuit." She wondered how babies could learn to talk properly if people confused them with stupid words like 'bikkie'. She stood by the window as she ate her biscuit. The curtains had been drawn this morning, but now she could see out into Mrs Cholsey's garden.

There was a little square yard at the back of the house, with a washing line. Flowers grew in fancy plastic pots on either side, and there was a tall hedge at the end. The yard was paved with squares of yellow and grey. They were uneven and the rain had made deep puddles. Stacey felt like going out and stamping in the puddles. A house with such a mean little garden was no better than a flat. Stacey liked throwing stones, but the garden was too small for that. There were no trees. Not even any earth to dig in.

Mrs Cholsey made a pot of tea.

"Take Timothy's cup up to him, will you?" she said to Stacey. "There's a good girl."

Timothy's room had a china sign saying 'Timmy's Room' and a notice written by Timothy saying 'Tres-passers will be eliminated', but the door was open, so Stacey took the tea in. Timothy was lying on his bed wearing headphones.

"Put it there," he said. Stacey put the cup down.

She looked around at the posters on the walls and the shelves full of games and toys.

"Thank you," said Timothy. "Goodbye." Stacey went downstairs. All the little children were drinking cups of tea. Mrs Cholsey was filling the babies' bottles with milky tea and screwing the tops on. She passed Stacey her cup.

"Sit down nicely while you drink it," she said. "We have to set the little ones a good example."

Stacey sat on the edge of the sofa and drank the tea. The television was on and the children sat and watched it. Mrs Cholsey held one of the babies on her lap and played games with it. It liked it when Mrs Cholsey pretended to eat its hand. The other baby wanted to play too, so Mrs Cholsey sat one on each of her knees and bounced them until their heads bumped together and they cried.

At last Mum came to fetch Stacey. Two of the children had already gone home, and the babies were asleep on the sofa, so it seemed quite quiet.

"She has been as good as gold," said Mrs Cholsey. "And tomorrow we won't feel quite so shy, will we, Stacey?"

"How was your work?" Stacey asked her mum when they were outside. "I bet you are tired out."

"I am tired," said Mum. "But it's not a bad job. I will get used to it. How did you get on at Mrs Cholsey's?"

"It was all right," said Stacey. "I'll get used to it."

The next morning it seemed less strange to be getting up in the middle of the night. The rain had washed away the mist, and washed down a lot of loose leaves from the trees as well. Stacey thought it was quite nice to have so much clear brown air to themselves, and not have to share it with smelly cars and noisy people.

"You don't mind going to the child-minder, do you?" asked Mum. "I expect it feels strange for you."

Stacey thought it was a bit late for Mum to ask that.

"I don't mind," she said. "Mrs Cholsey is too busy getting Timothy ready for school to get in a panic over my hair and my homework and all that, like you used to. So long as those babies don't expect too much of me, I shall be all right."

Stacey was not sure whether she was less nervous than the first day, because of knowing what to expect, or more nervous, because of knowing what to expect. She did worry that she would have to pick up a baby and that it might cry or be sick. She worried that Timothy might be horrible to her.

And she was worried about the other girl from her school called Karen. She thought it would be very embarrassing if Karen knew her and she did not know Karen. She tried to think of things to say to her that would sound as though she really did know her. But it turned out not to matter.

"Hello," said Karen, when she arrived. "Are you sure you go to my school? I have never seen you before in my life. Which class are you in?"

"Mrs Ebbs'," said Stacey. She noticed something hooked over Karen's ear. It must be a hearing aid. She wondered whether Karen would be able to hear what she said. "You are in Mr Iffley's, aren't you?"

"No," said Karen. "Miss Kidling's. You must be older than me. Are you going to be here every day?"

"Yes," said Stacey. "My mum started work at the hospital yesterday. She will be picking me up after she finishes at four."

"Is she a doctor?" asked Karen. "I bet she was nervous starting a new job."

"She is not a doctor," said Stacey. "She takes dinners round to all the wards and gives the patients their cups of tea. And she does some of the cleaning. I never thought about her being nervous. I was too busy being nervous myself about coming here."

"You are not nervous now, are you?" asked Karen. "It is all right here. Only you need to bring a book or something because Timothy won't let you touch his things." Karen spoke in a low voice, but Timothy was watching the television and ignoring the younger children. When one of the babies came and sat on his feet, he lifted his legs just enough to tip it off without even looking round.

"It's great after school," said Karen. "They have a fantastic garden. But Mrs Cholsey won't let us out there in the mornings in case we get ourselves muddy before school. Wait till this afternoon and I'll show you."

Stacey peered out of the window at the garden. It looked as dull as yesterday, only it was not raining and there were no puddles. Mrs Cholsey's washing was hanging on the line. Stacey thought that Karen must live in an even smaller flat than hers, if she was so excited about the little yard.

Karen got some pens and paper out of her school bag and they played heads-bodies-and-legs until it was time to leave for school. When they put their coats on, the babies got very excited. They shook the playpen and nearly shouted 'Bye-bye'.

Karen ran back and gave them both a kiss. One of them banged her on both ears and the other one licked her nose.

"Ugh," said Stacey, as they went out into the street. "Did that hurt?"

"Aren't they nice?" said Karen.

"Now, walk with Timothy," said Mrs Cholsey, "and he will take you safely across the roads. I'll be there when you come out. All right, Stacey? You will be all right, won't you?"

"I'll be fine," said Stacey, and they set off towards school. Timothy ran on ahead.

"Timothy's mum thinks he takes me to school every day," said Karen. "But he told me the very first day that he wouldn't walk with me. I don't mind. I don't want to walk with him either. By the way," she added, going a little pink, "you don't have to talk to me in school, you know. At dinner, I mean, or play-time."

"Why shouldn't I?" asked Stacey. "I was glad to see you this morning. You stopped me feeling nervous."

"Well," explained Karen, "Timothy just ignores. me while we are at school. So I thought, being older than me, you might not want to know me."

"I am not that old," said Stacey.

"See you later, then," said Karen.

When Stacey followed Karen out into the garden, she still could not see why Karen was so enthusiastic about it. She hopped a few times in the paving-stone squares and wondered whether Mrs Cholsey would let her draw on them with chalk. She wandered along the row of flowerpots, wondering whether some of the flowers were very unusual.

"Stacey!" called Karen. "Come and look at this!"

"Where are you?" asked Stacey. Karen was nowhere to be seen.

"Through here," said Karen, and Stacey saw her face looking through a gap in the hedge.

"What is behind there?" she asked.

"This is the garden," said Karen. "That part is just where they hang their washing. The real garden is through here."

There was a narrow pathway through the hedge that Stacey had not noticed. Beyond it the path wound across a lawn edged with tangled clumps of flowers, through trees covered in red apples, past a vegetable patch and another lawn to a high bank. A rope swing hung from one of the trees. Karen was standing on the top of the bank.

"Come up here," said Karen. "We can go on the swing later. It is a lovely garden, isn't it?"

"I never guessed it would be like this," said Stacey. "I thought it was just the yard. It's the longest garden I have ever seen. And the house looks so ordinary from the front."

"You haven't seen the best bit yet," said Karen.

"Isn't this the end of the garden, where the bank is?" asked Stacey.

"Yes," said Karen. "But come and look over the other side."

Stacey clambered up the bank. There were footholds in its grassy side where other people had climbed up before. When she reached the top she stood next to Karen, leaning against the little white-painted fence that ran along the top of the Cholseys' stretch of the bank. Below the bank on the other side was a footpath and beyond the path was water. There were ducks on it and swans, and tied to posts along the bank were small boats.

"Is this the same river that goes under that bridge on the High Street?" asked Stacey.

"I don't know," said Karen. "But one day I'm going to take that boat and row all the way up that way and see where it comes from. Then I'll row all the way back the other way and see where it goes."

There was no grassy bank on the far side of the

river. A high concrete wall dropped straight down into the water. The lower part of it was covered in green slime. There were some huge dark rusted rings let into the concrete, that boats could tie up to. Further along, metal loops were set in the concrete, one above the other like a ladder all the way up the wall. You could not see what was on the other side of the wall. It was too high.

The water lapped nicely against the grass by the path, and bobbed the little boats up and down. On the other side, the water looked less friendly. It sucked up against the wall and left the green shining as it slid away again. On this side you could see down to bricks and pebbles under the water, but the water by the wall was thick and brown. Stacey threw a stone over to the far side. She thought she could tell from the sound it made that the water was very deep.

"It must go down to the sea one way," she said.

"Down there," said Karen, pointing to their right. "You can see the water flowing that way. Look, the ducks drift that way when they forget to swim. But it is miles to the sea."

"Do you know how to row?" asked Stacey.

"It's easy," said Karen. "That boat is Timothy's own boat. He never uses it. It is just wasted. But if he can row, I am sure I can. One day I shall try it. The oars are in the garden shed." Timothy's boat was a little orange dinghy. It looked very shiny and new.

"Stacey!" They heard Mrs Cholsey calling. "Karen! Come on in now! Your mummies will be here in a minute."

Stacey took a last look at the river and the little boats tied up along its side, then slid down the bank into the garden. They had a quick turn each on the swing and hurried indoors.

"You like playing out of doors, do you?" asked Mrs Cholsey. "Just be careful to keep away from the water. It is such a nuisance. I can't let these little ones out there on their own for fear they will tumble in. We have got a fence along the end there, but it's only wooden palings and I'm afraid they might squeeze through. You really can't risk it when it's other people's children, can you? Not that we used to take the risk with Timothy. Mr Cholsey put wire netting along there, five foot high, but he thought it spoilt the outlook from the orchard, so he took it down once Timothy was big enough to be sensible. Now rub your feet on the mat and come and sit down quietly until your mothers are here."

The babies were sitting in a row on the sofa, watching the television. Timothy was lying on the floor.

"Was it very boring?" asked Mum, when she picked Stacey up at half past four. "Do you all just sit in front of the television all the time?"

"We went out in the garden today," said Stacey. "It is the best garden you have ever seen. It just isn't like Mrs Cholsey at all. There is a swing and apple trees, and two different lawns to play on and a secret path. I shall play out there every afternoon."

She did not mention the river.

One morning Mum asked Mrs Cholsey if Stacey could stay a little later than usual in the afternoon. She had to see the dentist straight from work.

"Good," said Karen. "You will be here for longer, then. Let's make it today that we try out the boat."

Stacey was shocked. She had never thought that Karen really meant to go out in Timothy's boat, and she didn't think that they should use it without asking, even if Timothy was not a very nice person. Besides, if they did ask, Timothy would probably say no, which would suit Stacey very well.

"We can't," she said. "Mrs Cholsey will call us after five minutes, and if we don't come in, she will come looking for us."

"I will tell her we are playing camps," said Karen. "She let me have my tea outside once. We'll ask for biscuits to eat out there and she will never guess that we are half way down to the sea."

"But we don't know how to row," said Stacey. "Suppose we get half way to the sea and can't steer it back again? Suppose a big wave comes and we capsize?"

"Just for the first time," said Karen, "I will row, and you can walk along the side of the river. Then if I get into trouble, I can throw you the rope and you can pull me ashore. The river is not very wide and I will keep close to the bank."

"I am older," said Stacey. "It should be me taking the risks."

"But you don't want to," said Karen. "And I do." Which was true.

After school, Karen asked Mrs Cholsey for some biscuits to take down the garden.

"Playing camps again, are you?" said Mrs Cholsey. "All right, I'll let you stay down there until five, seeing as your mummy is coming late today, Stacey. But keep your coats on because it's chilly these evenings. And try not to get too dirty. I don't like sending you home looking like a dog's dinner."

They found the oars in the garden shed. There was a heavy pair of wooden oars, and a pair of small plastic paddles.

"I will use the little ones," said Karen. "The wooden ones look more real, but these will be easier."

"Do you think we should?" asked Stacey. It felt almost like stealing.

"Yes, I think so," said Karen. "Those wooden ones are really heavy."

She climbed up the bank and Stacey passed the oars up to her. Then they clambered over the fence, slid down the other side of the bank and dropped the oars into the orange dinghy. It was the first time that Stacey had been so close to the river. The water was brown. In the dusk you could not see the bottom.

"It is very deep," said Stacey. "Can you swim, Karen?"

"Stop worrying," said Karen. "It's only a tiny river. Hardly bigger than a stream, really. And if I can't manage the oars, I will just throw the rope to you and you can pull me back."

She sat on the bank and lowered herself into the dinghy. It wobbled and she looked very unsteady.

"Just sit in it," suggested Stacey. "You really are afloat on the water. There is no need to untie it. It would be much safer."

But Karen was determined to row down the river. She sat on the little plank seat in the middle of the dinghy and fitted the oars into the rowlocks on each side.

"Cast off!" she called.

Stacey reluctantly began to untie the blue nylon rope that held the dinghy to the post on the shore.

"Don't row too far," she said, "will you? Supposing a fast motor boat comes and crashes into you, or wild geese attack you? It's not really very safe."

The rope was untied, but Stacey kept hold of the end of it. Karen began to drift away from the bank. She tried pulling on one of the oars. The boat turned a little. It was moving slowly downstream.

"You will have to let go of the rope," said Karen.

"It is pulling me to the side."

Already the dinghy was moving quite fast. Stacey walked alongside it on the bank. There was a narrow path along the edge of the river. There were clumps of nettles, and in places trees and brambles stretched out over the path, but Stacey kept her eyes on the little boat. She felt that she could keep it from sinking if she watched it hard enough. Some nettles stung her legs.

"Throw the rope to me," said Karen. "I want to row properly."

"You are rowing very well," said Stacey. She was still holding the rope.

"Don't worry about me," said Karen. "I can row to the shore if I need to. Look, it is easy. Let go of the rope."

Suddenly there was a shout from up the river, where they had come from.

"Hey! Get out of that boat!"

It was Timothy. Stacey kept her grip on the rope. Karen pulled the oars into the boat. Timothy made his way cautiously down the path. When he reached Stacey he snatched the rope from her and pulled the boat in towards the shore.

"Get out," he said to Karen. "Thief."

"We are not thieves," said Karen. "We don't want to steal your boat. We were just trying it out. It doesn't look as though you have ever used it at all. We weren't doing any harm."

Stacey stretched out a hand to pull Karen up the

bank, but as Karen got one foot on the bank, Timothy bent down and gripped the side of the boat.

"Think you know about boats, do you?" he jeered, and he rocked the boat, first gently and then harder and harder. Karen had one foot in the boat and one on the bank, and could not move. Stacey thought Karen would split in half or fall in the river as Timothy pushed the side of the dinghy down nearly into the water and then let it swing up again. She wanted to get hold of him and make him stop, but he was big enough to knock her and Karen both into the water. She got hold of Karen's hand and helped to keep her steady as the boat rocked under her, and then when the side of the boat was down, Karen jumped ashore, holding tight to Stacey so that they nearly fell.

Timothy did not say another word. He pulled the boat, like a dog on a lead, all the way back along the edge of the river. Karen and Stacey followed him at a little distance. Stacey wanted to get back indoors, away from the water. Out here, out of sight of the house, Timothy could do anything to them. He could give them just a little push, almost without meaning to, and they would be in the brown water. In the dark, he could almost pretend not to have seen them fall.

As soon as they reached the end of Mrs Cholsey's garden, Stacey started to clamber up the bank with Karen close behind her.

"Just a minute," said Timothy.

They stopped and looked back at him.

"Put the oars away," he said, "and we'll say no

more about you borrowing the boat." Stacey took a deep breath. Timothy was not planning to push them into the water, or even to tell his mother that they had been in his boat. She gave a small, grateful smile.

Then, as Timothy climbed up the bank and swung his leg over the fence at the top, he called over his shoulder, "Meet me here tomorrow. I'll take you for a real boat trip. But don't breathe a word to anyone, or your lives won't be worth living." He climbed up the bank and disappeared over the other side.

Stacey looked at Karen. They slid back down the bank to fetch the oars.

"I don't want to go in the boat with him," said Stacey. "He'll rock it to frighten us, or he'll push us off in it with no oars. He nearly drowned you back there. I hate him."

"It will be all right," said Karen. "It is his boat, after all. I expect he knows how to row it, and he just wants to show off. Children don't really drown each other, and it isn't worth having him for an enemy."

"He couldn't really do anything to us if we didn't go with him," said Stacey.

"He could tell his mother about us taking the boat," said Karen. "Then she would never let us outside again and we would have to watch television for the rest of our lives. You can have a bad cold and stay indoors tomorrow if you like. I don't mind."

"No," said Stacey, "I'll come too. I don't want to, but I will."

Indoors, with the lights on, you could imagine that

there was nothing beyond the little yard. No orchard, no dark river and no dinghy. Stacey and Karen sat quietly down in front of the television. Timothy was not there. One of the babies climbed on to Karen's lap and stroked her face.

"You are nice," said Karen sadly. Stacey reached out and pulled the other baby on to her lap. It was useful to have something to hug.

Mum seemed so calm in the morning, getting ready for work. She wore her plainest clothes and her flattest shoes and packed her overall in her bag.

"I promised to take in a photograph of you," she told Stacey. "One of the patients keeps asking about you. She's a nice old thing, and she has got no family of her own. I am not supposed to talk to the patients really. The tea-trolley and the floors are supposed to take up all my time. But the poor old dear doesn't have much to make her life worth living. I'll take in your school photograph. It will just fit into my bag."

"I feel sick," said Stacey.

"Oh, Stacey!" said Mum, and Stacey could see that Mum was worrying about who would look after her all day, as well as feeling sorry for her. "Do you really, love?"

"No," said Stacey. "Not really."

"I hope that milk was all right," said Mum. "It has been in the fridge for two days. Did it taste funny?"

"No," said Stacey. "It was fine. I am all right. Let's go."

"You don't really mind going to Mrs Cholsey's, do you?" asked Mum as they went downstairs. "Not now that you are used to her? There are other children there about your age, aren't there?"

"Yes," said Stacey. "It's all right."

"There's that little girl from your school, isn't there?" said Mum. "She looks nice. And how old is Mrs Cholsey's son? Is he a bit too old to play with you?"

"Yes," said Stacey. "Have you got the photograph? Tell the old lady I hope she gets better soon."

Timothy was eating breakfast when they reached Mrs Cholsey's house, and Stacey had to sit down opposite him. He looked like a quite ordinary boy as he scooped cornflakes into his mouth and drank his tea. Stacey told herself that it was not surprising that he had been angry when they took his boat, or that he had decided to punish Karen by rocking the boat and frightening her. He was an ordinary boy who was looking forward to showing off how good at rowing he was.

But even if Timothy was the best rower in the world and did not plan to leave Stacey and Karen adrift on the river or tip them into the murky water, Stacey still dreaded the boat trip he had promised them. The boat was so small and wobbly, and the river was so dark. Stacey imagined that once you fell under the water you would not know which way was up and which way was down.

She thought of eels slithering by, and how horrible

even clear blue water had felt in her nose and throat when she had once fallen into the swimming pool. She used to be able to swim. Probably her arms and legs still knew how to but they never had the chance now, and she did not want to try them out.

"Not hungry this morning?" said Mrs Cholsey. "Come along, my duck, eat up your cereal and I can wash the bowls. Look, here is Karen." She went to the front door to let Karen in.

The babies seemed noisier than ever. The boy baby threw his tortoise for Stacey to fetch. Stacey gave it back to him. He waved it at her and accidentally hit her on the nose with it. Tears came to her eyes and the baby laughed. It was a terrible morning.

On the way to school, Karen and Stacey did not talk. At school it was difficult to concentrate and Stacey was told off for day-dreaming. She thought it was more like day-nightmaring. She kept imagining Timothy rocking the boat with her and Karen in it, pushing it away from the bank and leaving it to float down to the sea.

"We are just going into the garden," Karen told Mrs Cholsey in the afternoon. "We won't get dirty."

"Don't go near the water, will you," said Mrs Cholsey. "One of these days I'll ask Mr Cholsey to take you out in the dinghy, but you must never touch it without a grown-up there. Do you know, it has hardly been used since we bought it? Timothy has never learnt to swim, so I can't let him in it on his own. His father took him for a row once or twice, but he has never shown any interest. Just play in the garden, there's good girls."

Outside, Karen whispered to Stacey, "So he doesn't know how to row, then. What do you think he means to do?"

They walked slowly through the garden, and climbed the bank. Timothy was sitting in the dinghy, smiling at them. Stacey tried to work out what sort of smile it was.

"All aboard!" he called. "This is going to be exciting!"

Stacey and Karen stood on the path and looked down at him.

"Come on," said Timothy. "I won't do anything stupid. I was just angry yesterday. But when I saw that you two little kids could manage the boat, I decided to have a go myself. Get in, I won't make it rock."

"We couldn't really manage it," said Stacey. "I was holding on to the rope all the time, so that I could pull Karen back. The river was pulling her along quite fast. I don't think she could have rowed back by herself."

"I'm strong," said Timothy. "Get in."

Karen stepped into the dinghy. With two people in it, it was quite low in the water.

"Where shall I sit?" asked Karen.

"In the front," said Timothy. Karen climbed over the plank seat and arranged her legs in the small triangle at the front of the boat. When Timothy turned to look at her, the boat tipped and a little water lapped over the bow.

"She had better get out," said Stacey. "Look, it is going to sink."

"We are not balanced quite right," said Timothy. "Come and sit at the back, Karen. Then the boat will be flatter in the water."

Karen climbed back over the seat and carefully lowered herself on to the floor, but this time the boat swung the other way and she stood up quickly.

"I will have to sit next to you," she said. "I am big for my age. That's why I am so heavy."

Timothy moved over and they sat together on the seat in the middle of the boat, with an oar each. There was no room for Stacey, which was a relief.

"Let me hold the rope," she said, "until you are sure you can row it all right."

But Timothy had to show that he could manage better than Karen had done the day before. He untied the rope himself and pulled it into the boat. Then he took hold of his oar and ordered Karen, "Pull – now!"

The two oars dipped into the water and the boat began to move. The river pulled it slowly along anyway, but with each pull on the oars it turned to one side or the other. Once it turned right round so that it was travelling backwards downstream.

"Can't you pull steadily?" said Timothy crossly. "When I tell you. Now, pull!"

Some ducks flew up from the bank of the river just beneath Stacey's feet.

"Where are you going to row to?" called Stacey. "Don't go too far. It will be harder work coming back." She was not at all sure that they would be able even to turn round when they wanted to. She was certain that they would not be able to row home against the current. It would be hard work pulling them back with the rope. Perhaps one of them would get out and help.

They went further than Karen had gone the day before. They worked out how to keep the boat facing the right way. They went round a bend in the river so that their own mooring-post was out of sight. On the far side of the river there was a gap in the high concrete wall. A narrow stone staircase climbed up out of the water in the gap. The steps looked slippery. Stacey hated the way the water slapped up against them. She shivered.

"You are good at rowing," Stacey called half-heartedly. She hoped that Timothy would feel he had shown them how clever he was, and would stop.

"It gets easier as you go along," said Timothy. "Doesn't it, Karen?"

Karen looked doubtful. She kept on dipping in her oar in time with Timothy's. "Well," she said, "we aren't going round and round. But I think rowing should be hard work, and this isn't hard at all. The river is doing all the work for us."

Round the bend in the river was a small island. It was just a few bushes and a tree on a muddy bank. There was an old swan's nest at one end of it.

"Watch out!" said Stacey. "The water is shallow on this side of the island. You will get stuck." She could see the reeds just below the surface.

"Pull, Karen," shouted Timothy. "Pull on your side. We will have to go the other way round the island."

Karen pulled and the little dinghy slowly disappeared behind the island. Suddenly Stacey heard someone shout. She was not sure whether it was Timothy or Karen. She watched for the dinghy to come out from the other side of the island. It was taking a long time.

"Are you all right?" she called.

"Stacey!" called Karen. "Come and help us quick!"

"What has happened?" Stacey shouted back. She could not see through the bushes on the island.

"We are shipwrecked," Karen shouted. "I think Timothy is hurt. He won't say anything."

Stacey heard Karen talking to Timothy, but she did not hear Timothy's voice.

"Is he in the water?" she called. "Did you fall out of the boat?"

"Just come and help!" shouted Karen. "I can't keep on holding him. I'll have to let the boat go."

The little orange dinghy, empty, floated out from behind the island, and spun slowly down the river.

"How can I come and help?" screamed Stacey. "I haven't got a boat, have I?"

There was no answer.

Stacey | CHAPTER TEN

Stacey knew that she would have to try to help, but walking into the water felt like stepping off the top of a cliff. She was not at all sure that she would be any help to the others, or even that she would still be alive in ten minutes' time, but she did not have a choice. She took off her shoes and coat first.

"Come on," shouted Karen. "I can't keep hold of him."

"I am coming," called Stacey.

She stepped down into the water. It was freezing. She wondered how long it would take to die of cold. The water was so cold that it hurt her like a burn as it touched each new part of her legs. She could feel slime and mud through her socks. Her smart school skirt got wet and filled with air like a balloon. She wished she had taken it off too. When she pushed the air out of it, it stuck to her legs and wrapped itself round them.

The next step took her in up to her waist. She thought the cold would stop her breathing. There were reeds all round her. She could already imagine how the water would taste if she fell into it, and she could feel it swishing inside her head. She tried to take long steps, and kept herself steady by paddling through the water with her hands as she walked. Something brushed against her legs. She felt sick. She wished she could just close her eyes and not have to notice what would happen next.

"Don't worry," she called to Karen. "It will be all right. I am half way over to the island."

She made the mistake of looking down. She could see her legs disappearing into the dark water. She could see the pale reeds swaying. It made her giddy, and she clutched at a handful of water to keep herself upright. She fell against the muddy side of the island and scrambled up.

On the other side, a branch of the tree had half broken off and fallen across the water. It looked too high to have hit the dinghy, but perhaps it had just caught Timothy's head and knocked them off balance. Karen was kneeling in the water with her arms around Timothy. Timothy did not look drowned. In fact his hair was not completely wet. But he was up to his shoulders in the water and was not moving at all. The water was flowing quite fast on this side of the island, and it was tugging at Timothy.

"Help me," said Karen. "He is so heavy. The water is trying to pull him away."

"What is the matter with him?" asked Stacey. She clambered down and grabbed one of Timothy's arms. "He isn't dead." They pulled him up out of the water.

"He stood up," said Karen, "and I think the tree banged him. But it didn't bang him very hard. It knocked him over, and he tried to jump on to the island, and then the boat tipped up. I think he is just too frightened to move."

Stacey dragged Timothy further up the muddy side of the island. She looked into his face, and she could tell that he could see her. She shook him.

"There is only one way to get back," she said. "And sitting in the river isn't it."

Timothy opened his mouth. "I can't swim," he whispered.

"Can't swim and can't row," said Karen. "This is a great time to tell us that."

"You don't need to swim," said Stacey. "I walked over here. We will hold on to you. It's easy as long as you don't think about it. Get up."

Timothy got up. It was strange to see such a big boy shaking and crying. Karen and Stacey took hold of him by a hand each and led him through the bushes to the other side of the island.

"Are you all right, Karen?" asked Stacey.

"I'm cross," said Karen, her teeth chattering. "This boy is useless. He has got us all wet and freezing, and my gran will kill me if I have got water in my hearing aid. I don't suppose Mrs Cholsey will ever let us out of her sight again."

They led Timothy through the reeds to the bank where Stacey had left her shoes. It was not frightening for Stacey on the way back. She was too busy to notice the slime underfoot or the way the water sucked at her legs as she pushed her way through it. When they reached the bank Timothy just stood in the water holding the two girls' hands.

"You will have to climb up," said Stacey. "We can't lift you all the way up there."

Timothy crawled up the bank and sat shaking on the path.

Karen looked at him. "We can't take you home like this. Your mother would have a heart attack. What is the matter with you, anyway? You fell in the water and got a bit wet. Stacey and I stopped you from floating down to the sea. You walked to the edge and got out. Now what is the matter?"

Timothy covered his face in his hands. Stacey rubbed his wet shoulders. She thought it must be very hard for him not to be the biggest and toughest and cleverest any more.

When he looked up he was not crying any more. He gave his head a shake, then stood up and shook his arms and legs as though he was getting the creases out of them.

"Thanks," he said.

Karen had walked further down the river.

"It's here!" she called. "It's stuck in these reeds. I think I can get it."

"Leave it," said Stacey. "I never want to see it again. I just want to get warm."

Karen was stretching out into the reeds. She stood up with the rope in her hand and pulled the dinghy in to the bank.

They emptied the water out of the dinghy and hurried back along the path. Their clothes stuck to their legs and arms. Stacey ached all over with the cold. She remembered wading into the river, expecting to die of slime if not of drowning, and it seemed a very long time ago. She looked sideways at Timothy. He did not look frightened any more, or ashamed. He just looked tired. And Karen looked annoyed. She was pulling the boat along fiercely, getting cross with it when the rope stuck on clumps of weeds on the river bank.

They tied up the boat in its proper place as though it had never been used.

When Stacey's mum arrived, Timothy was upstairs in bed with a hot water bottle. Stacey and Karen were dressed in some of Timothy's old clothes. Mrs Cholsey had put them both in the bath and washed their hair. The bath water ended up cloudy with mud and rather green.

"I have put her clothes in a plastic bag," Mrs Cholsey told Stacey's mum. "I rinsed out the worst of it, and I think they will wash out all right. I'd have done it myself, only there were the babies to feed. They were in a proper mess, and I'm afraid I didn't have any spare clothes the right size for her. I've plenty for the little ones, they are always wetting themselves or getting in a mess, but Stacey has had to make do with my Timothy's things."

The bottoms of Timothy's trousers were rolled up to fit Stacey's legs. His old t-shirt fitted her, and his socks, but the jumper was rather baggy. She was wearing his old teddy-bear slippers.

"I can't say how sorry I am," Mrs Chosley said.

"Mind you, it couldn't have happened if they had taken notice of me and kept away from the water, but I suppose I have to be thankful that the girls were there or Timothy might never have got out. I must have told him a hundred times not to go past the fence. I don't know what can have come over him. Of course I keep an eye on them when they are out in the garden, but I can't be everywhere all at once."

"No," said Mum. "Of course not. And Stacey is big enough to know better than to play by the edge of the river."

Mrs Cholsey seemed relieved.

"I wonder if we shall see you tomorrow," she said to Stacey. "I shouldn't be surprised if all three of you went down with colds."

Mum peeped into the plastic bag as they walked home.

"They still look very slimy," she said. "Horrible. You will have to wash them out as soon as we get home or the skirt will never be dry for school tomorrow. It is lucky you have two school jumpers."

"I haven't got to wash them, have I?" said Stacey. "Mothers are supposed to do all that. And you should put me to bed with some nice hot cocoa and speak soothingly to me. That is what Mrs Cholsey was doing to Timothy."

She walked on as quickly as she could, hoping that no-one would see her in the baggy jumper and silly slippers.

"I will speak soothingly to you while you wash the

clothes," said Mum, "if that will make you feel better. But if you get yourself all slimy, you can get yourself all unslimy too. Maybe if Mrs Cholsey wasn't quite such a perfect mother, Timothy would be able to look after himself a bit better and not need rescuing. What happened exactly? Mrs Cholsey seemed to think that he nearly drowned himself, and you and Karen heroically dived in to save him. Is that right?"

Stacey thought for a while.

"It didn't happen exactly the way we told Mrs Cholsey," she said. "Just as we were starting to tell her what happened, Timothy butted in. He told her that he had fallen in the river and that Karen and I pulled him out. And it was his fault really, so that was fair."

"Was it partly your fault as well?" asked Mum. "It is none of my business really, what you do when I am not looking after you. But I don't want you to do anything dangerous. Not very dangerous, anyway."

"It certainly was not my fault," said Stacey indignantly. "I wasn't even in the boat!"

Mum stared at her. Stacey remembered that no-one had mentioned the boat to Mrs Cholsey or Mum. She wished she had not said anything about it. The story that Timothy had told his mother about him just falling in off the bank was much simpler.

"I didn't want the others to go in it," Stacey said. She told Mum what had happened. "But anyway, Mum, I think we should go swimming again, just for practice, in case I ever need to rescue anyone else. I only had to wade today, but next time it might be deeper."

"I should think you'd better start using a bit of sense as well," said Mum. "Don't you know that's how kids get drowned, playing by rivers and canals, and messing about in boats that they can't control?" They walked on in silence, Stacey shuffling the teddy-bear slippers.

"Was Mrs Cholsey angry," asked Mum, "when you all came in dripping wet?"

"Not as much as I thought she would be," said Stacey. "But I think she was in such a panic about Timothy's chest getting frozen that she forgot to be angry. And when Timothy told her that we had rescued him she was terribly grateful. It is the first good thing he has done. You should be worried about my chest, you know, Mum. That water was colder than ice. I don't know why it wasn't frozen solid."

As they went upstairs to their flat, Mum began to laugh. Stacey looked at her.

"It's nothing, really," said Mum. "It's just that I was afraid you were bored at Mrs Cholsey's. I felt so sorry for you, sitting in front of the television every afternoon. From now on, that will be the least of my worries."

Part Three | Timothy

Timothy | CHAPTER ONE

Timothy held the tent-pegs while his father struggled to lay the tent out flat on the lawn. The tent was an ugly light green. Timothy thought it was a colour that you never found in leaves or grass or sea, only in plastic school dinner-plates or swimming-pool walls.

"It's all a question of doing things in the right order," said his father. "Assemble the poles, Tim. No, put those pegs down first. Not there, boy! They'll get lost! Lay them out on the path. Now, the poles."

Timothy found the metal sections of the tent-poles. There were six of them. He looked at them helplessly.

"Aha!" said his father. "Initiative test!" He sat back on his heels and watched as Timothy tried to fit two pieces of pole together. They were the same size and would not go together. He picked another two. One fitted into the other, and a third went onto that. Timothy found a fourth piece and fitted it on the end. His father leant forward and snatched the poles from him.

"Idiot!" he snapped. "What are you trying to make?

A fishing rod?" He quickly took off the fourth section, slid the last pieces together and held out a pair of tent-poles, each made of three sections. Timothy took them and wondered what he was supposed to do with them.

"Well?" asked his father. "You've got the tent. You've got the poles. What are you going to do next?"

Timothy knelt down and fumbled under the heavy green canvas, trying to poke the top of one of the poles through a metal ring in the middle of the tent. It was like trying to thread a needle with gloves on. He got it through at last and laid it down carefully to start on the other. While he was doing that, the first one fell out of its hole. He thought it would be easier if his father would hold up the tent while he crawled under with the poles. Then they could stand them upright, which would stop them falling out of their holes. But his father was enjoying watching him.

"Just as well you haven't got a force ten gale raging around you," said his father. "Eh, Tim?"

Timothy thought that he would have more sense than to go camping in a force ten gale. In fact, if he had the choice, he would not go camping at all. He climbed under the canvas, stood the poles upright with their ends through the two holes, and crept out backwards, holding the canvas steady as he went.

He wondered what was supposed to keep the poles standing upright. Was it all done with the tent-pegs?

"Guy-ropes next," said his father. "I'll hold the poles steady."

Timothy looked around for the guy-ropes. There were two thin orange strings lying on the grass. He picked one up and saw that it had a loop at each end.

"Come on, boy," said his father. "Don't take all day." He reached out to take the string from Timothy, and by mistake let go of the tent so that it fell down in a heap. Timothy felt scared. His father got angriest when he made mistakes himself.

"Don't just stand there!" his father shouted. "Can't you do anything without being told how?"

Timothy dived down under the canvas again. One of the poles had come apart and he tried to fit it together in the green darkness. When he had got the poles upright again and made his way out, his father had disappeared. Timothy wondered how they would manage the tent in a field. He reached down for the guy-rope, hooked it over the top of the peg and wondered what the other end should be fastened to.

He stood there wondering, and noticed that there were two clouds above the house that looked exactly like a bed chasing a crocodile. Just then, his mother came out of the house, carrying one of the babies, and the crocodile fell in half.

"You should be up in your room keeping warm," said Mrs Cholsey. It was not really cold in spite of the clouds. "I only kept you off school so that you could get over that throat of yours."

"He told me to come out and help with the tent," said Timothy.

"Don't call your father 'he'," said Mrs Cholsey.

"Ups-a-daisy!" she said to the baby she was carrying. "Is that a silly Timmy, then? Oh, you are getting heavy. I hope your mummy isn't late fetching you today. She's cried every time I've put her down. Maybe she's coming down with your germs, Timothy. That's another good reason for you to be out of the way upstairs."

Timothy went indoors. Mr Cholsey was in the living room pretending to watch the television. It was a programme about some sort of illness, so Timothy knew he was not really watching it. The little children that Mrs Cholsey looked after while their parents were working were being very quiet and good. Mr Cholsey was always in a bad mood when he had time off work, because he did not like Mrs Cholsey having all the children in the house. Usually he did not have to see them, and Mrs Cholsey made sure that the toys and bottles and pushchairs were out of the way when he got home from work.

Timothy walked quietly through the living room to the hall.

"Given up already?" said Mr Cholsey. Timothy thought that was unfair because his father was the one who had given up first.

"Mummy wanted me to come indoors," said Timothy. He waited, in case his father was going to tell him to go out again and carry on with the tent.

"Well, don't just stand there," said Mr Cholsey. One of the little children wandered across in front of the television. "Can't even watch the television in peace," he muttered. Timothy went upstairs. He wished he had gone to school.

He sat at the desk in his room and picked up a piece of card that was lying on it. He folded it in two to make it into a tent. He found a red sweet paper. Crumpled up, it could be a camp fire. He took a clean sock out of his drawer for a sleeping bag. He bent to peep into the tent and wondered who could fit in it.

Mrs Cholsey came in, still carrying the baby.

"I've brought your hot lemon drink, dear," she said. "Now, what a mess! Sweet papers, dirty socks, goodness me!"

She swept the tent and camp fire into the waste-paper bin and put the sleeping bag in her apron pocket. The baby pulled it out and threw it at Timothy. Timothy lay back on the bed and closed his eyes. He did not feel ill, but it hardly seemed worth the bother of being well.

Timothy | CHAPTER TWO

At four o'clock Karen and Stacey came in from school. Timothy could hear them talking and laughing downstairs. He did not dare go down to see them because the noise would be making his father crosser and crosser. It was strange that both the girls were a little afraid of his father, but neither knew how to behave so as not to annoy him. Timothy called quietly down the stairs.

"Stacey! Karen! Do you want to play upstairs?"

There was no answer. It was quiet downstairs. Then Timothy heard their voices through his window. They had gone out into the garden. He leant his head against the glass and watched them. They were looking at the tent spread out on the grass.

"They know I'm ill," thought Timothy angrily. "They could have come up just to see me." He lay back on the bed again and picked up his drawing book. "I expect they will try to put up the tent. Stupid girls."

He drew a picture of the tent, with four legs,

Karen's and Stacey's, sticking out from under it. He drew the tent with a nasty face showing in its folds, wrapping itself round the girls and tying them up with its guy-ropes. Then he made a flash of lightning strike the tent monster, because Karen and Stacey were not enemies and he didn't really want to leave them in such a tangle. He wouldn't mind being friends with them, if only they would think of him as a person. He wished they had noticed his flash of lightning rescuing them.

The next time he looked out of the window, the tent was up. It sagged in the middle, but it was standing up, and the bottom was spread out and held in place with the tent pegs. Timothy thought it was unfair that his father should have put the tent up for Karen and Stacey, when he wouldn't help Timothy with it at all. It was unfair, even though Timothy did not want the tent up.

The side of the tent was bulging. Someone was moving about inside. There were squeaking noises from down in the garden. While Timothy watched, four of Mrs Cholsey's little children came crawling out, followed by Karen. They crawled round the lawn, searching for something. Then they dived back into the tent. Stacey came out into the garden with a tray of drinks. She put it down by the tent flap and slid it inside. Then she disappeared too.

Timothy went down to the kitchen.

"The sun has come out," he told his mother. "I'm going outside."

"Are you, dear?" asked Mrs Cholsey. "You may as well have your drink out there, then. But make sure you come straight in if you feel it getting at all cool. Let me give you your medicine first. It must be about four hours since the last lot."

She spooned the medicine into Timothy's mouth, gave him a steaming cup and rocked the baby, who was chewing a wooden spoon and looking very sleepy in its bouncy chair. Mr Cholsey was snoring in the living room. Timothy carried his drink outside, but stopped for a minute outside the tent. Perhaps the others would not want him to play with them.

"It's my father's tent," he thought. "Not theirs. In fact they have no right to be in it at all." He lifted the flap, but could not get inside the tent because it was full of people's legs.

"No room, Timfy Pimfy," said one of the little children. "Go away."

"Don't be horrible," said Stacey. "You can move up. Alvin can sit on my lap. Come on in, Timothy."

"I thought you were ill," said Karen. "Your mother said you were ill in bed. You don't look very ill."

"It's my throat," said Timothy. "You wouldn't expect to be able to see that." Then he thought that there was no need to pretend to Karen. "Actually, I'm all right. My mother thinks I am ill, but there's nothing much wrong with me. Can I come in?" As he said it, he wondered why he was asking permission to go into his own father's tent.

Stacey moved the children along and Timothy sat

down next to Marcus, the one who had told him to go away. He had to bend to fit the sloping side of the tent. It was not comfortable, but it was cosier than the cardboard tent he had made. He sipped his drink.

"Are you drinking tea?" asked Karen. "I wouldn't fancy it in this weather. Too hot."

"It's lemon," said Timothy. "Supposed to be good for me."

"I want some," said Marcus, and stretched up for the cup.

"It's hot!" said Timothy. "Watch out!" He jerked the cup away from Marcus and the drink splashed out against the side of the tent, and ran away into the grass.

"I want lemon," said Marcus. "Stupid Timfy spilt it."

Timothy was about to protest that it was Marcus who had made it spill, but then he just said, "It wasn't very nice. Drink up your squash."

"I drinked it already," said Marcus, and shook his cup upside down to prove it. The last few drops splashed on to Timothy's legs. Stacey gave out biscuits and the children munched quietly. They all looked pale in the green light coming through the canvas sides of the tent. Timothy wondered whether they had been playing a game before he arrived. Perhaps he had interrupted it. Perhaps they were waiting for him to go away again. He ate his biscuit slowly, nibbling round the edge so that it stayed round.

Suddenly sunlight came in. Mr Cholsey had lifted the flap of the tent. He looked very surprised.

"So you got the tent up all right, then, Tim?" he said. "Well done, son."

Timothy opened his mouth to say that he hadn't put it up, but Karen reached behind Marcus and pinched Timothy's elbow very hard, so that he just squeaked instead.

"The guy-ropes could do with a bit of tightening," said Mr Cholsey. Only his head was showing between flaps of canvas. You could imagine that it was just hanging there, with nobody joined on to it. "But you've done a fine job. Be careful what you let the little ones get up to. I've had this tent since I was a boy, you know." The flap closed again. Karen turned round and peeped under the bottom of the tent.

"He's gone indoors again," she said.

"Why did you pinch me?" said Timothy. "I was just going to tell him that it wasn't me that put the tent up."

"I know," said Karen. "But he wanted it to be you who had done it. I thought we would do him a favour and let him go on thinking it really was you."

"I thought it was him that put it up for you," said Timothy.

"Karen put it up for me," said Marcus.

"Stacey put it for me," said Alvin.

"We put it up ourselves," said Stacey. "We got a bit tangled up, but it wasn't hard really."

"He tried to make me do it," said Timothy. "I'm

hopeless at things like that. It kept falling over. Mind you, he wasn't any better at it himself. That's why he's been sulking."

He peeped under the edge of the tent to check that his father was really indoors and not listening. He could see him back on the sofa reading the paper. He had never thought of his father as sulking before, because Mrs Cholsey always said, "Your father is tired", or, "Your father has one of his headaches", but he realised that if his father was a child, everyone would say that he was sulking.

"Get up," said Marcus. "You are squashing me, fat Timfy."

Timothy looked at him. "Why are you always nasty to me, Marcus?"

"Because you don't like me," said Marcus.

Timothy said nothing. He did not like Marcus very much, but perhaps it was not fair to dislike someone so very small. Marcus always wore such ugly smart little clothes, but that was probably not his fault.

"I suppose," said Stacey, "your father is pleased now, even though he hasn't put up the tent himself, because he thinks that he has trained you to do it. My mum is like that sometimes – she gets pleased when I do something, as though it was all her cleverness that had done it."

"The trouble is," said Timothy, "he will expect me to put the tent up again when we go camping and I won't be able to do it. And then if he can't do it either, we will be in a mess."

"We'll show you how," said Stacey. "If you just look at it now it's up, you can see how it goes."

"Are you really going camping?" asked Karen.

"All weekend," said Timothy gloomily. "I wish it would snow."

"You are lucky," said Karen. "I wish my dad would take me camping."

"Don't eat grass, Lucy," said Stacey.

"Why shouldn't she?" said Karen. "Greens are supposed to be good for you."

All the little children except Alvin began to pull up grass with their mouths. Alvin's mouth was already full of some of his fingers and a little piece of blanket.

"I'm a goat," said Marcus. "Grrrr!"

"Goats don't growl," said Karen. "And you'd better not eat it. We are supposed to be looking after you. Mrs Cholsey won't trust us with you if we let you get sick." The children took no notice.

"My mum and me went camping once," said Stacey. "Last summer, when it was really hot. We just took a plastic sheet to lie on and blankets, and we walked for miles, and then we slept out under the sky. We lay and looked at the stars for ages. It's the best thing I've ever done. But we didn't take enough food. I woke up in the middle of the night and ate all the breakfast, and then in the morning I was ready for another breakfast."

Timothy was horrified. "No tent?" he said. "No beds? My mum said I mustn't lie on the damp ground because of my chest, so my dad got camp beds for us.

The legs come off, and they roll up in a bundle. It must be really uncomfortable just on the ground."

"I'm going to practise tonight," said Karen. "I shall sleep on my bedroom floor. I wish we had a garden at home. You could sleep out every night, Timothy. We've got a flat roof next door to our flat, but I'm not allowed on it. It would be a good place for looking at stars."

"I wish my dad would take you camping instead of me," said Timothy. "I know what it will be like. He'll have all these ideas about what boys ought to have fun doing out in the country. He won't know what to do himself, and he'll get cross with me because I don't know either. Rubbing sticks together to make a fire and all that."

"I should think he would take some matches," said Stacey. "We did, but we never made a fire because everything was so dry we were afraid we wouldn't be able to put it out. You could take a box of matches yourself, couldn't you?"

"And take a tin-opener," said Karen, "in case he forgets it. That would make him angry. I know what you mean. My dad always gets in a temper when we go on a trip anywhere if everything doesn't go just as he plans. It was really funny when we went to the zoo. Do you remember I told you, Stacey, about the camel, and the fuss Dad made about those egg sandwiches?"

"Yes," said Stacey. "You'll have to tell us what happens, Timothy. Maybe your dad will be all relaxed and pleasant when he gets away from home. Some people are like that."

Timothy thought that his father was often relaxed but hardly ever pleasant. But he began to think that it might be fun to tell Karen and Stacey about the camping trip afterwards, and that if things did go wrong, there might be more stories to tell. It was nice in the tent, with the little ones crawling over his feet. But he remembered that Karen and Stacey had been playing in the tent before he arrived and perhaps they were still waiting for him to go.

He knelt up and filled the tray with the empty cups, then crawled backwards out of the tent and carried the tray into the kitchen.

Timothy went back to school the next day. It would have been a good day to be ill at home, because Mr Cholsey set off early to play golf. The baby who had been so miserable the day before did not come at all, and it was the day for Marcus and Alvin to go to play school, so the house would be quiet. But Mrs Cholsey looked into Timothy's throat, felt his forehead, noticed how much he ate for breakfast, and decided that he was well enough for school.

He thought of walking there with Stacey and Karen, but they left before he was ready and he never caught them up. He could not blame them, because he hardly ever waited for them. If one of them was missing, he usually walked with the other. Then he did not have to worry that they would rather be talking just to each other. When they were together they were so friendly that it made him uncomfortable. He thought they might joke together about him, about how he was scared of water and couldn't play marbles or put up tents.

They always walked home separately since Mrs Cholsey had decided they were old enough to walk home without her. Karen and Stacey came out of a different side of the school from Timothy and usually a few minutes earlier than him. Sometimes Timothy went the long way home, over the bridge. Today he stopped and looked down into the brown water.

He liked it better in winter when the river was full, and you could imagine the springs high up in the hills, or slopes of melting snow far away where the water was coming from. Sometimes he threw in sticks or paper boats and tried to remember them later in the evening, or the next morning, when they might have reached Tower Bridge, or got out to the open sea. More likely the sticks got stuck against the bank and the paper boats got soggy and sank. Anyway, in this dry weather the water seemed to go slowly and the bright sunshine showed up the mud and rubbish too clearly and spoilt the reflections.

Timothy was in no hurry to get home. His father would be back from playing golf, and by this time all the little children would be getting cross and tired and wanting biscuits and attention.

"There's Timfy!"

Timothy looked up. His mother was pushing the babies home from the shops. Marcus was running ahead and had seen him on the bridge.

"Silly Timfy!" he shouted. But he looked pleased to see Timothy. He came running on as though he was going to hug Timothy, but he stopped short, gave a crooked smile and kicked Timothy on the leg. Timothy thought that if he could swing Marcus up into the air, or even pat his head convincingly, they might be friends. But Marcus was wearing a nasty little peaked cap which made it difficult to pat his head. By the time Timothy had thought about it, it was too late anyway, and Marcus was dropping pebbles through the railings into the water. He was probably trying to hit the duck that had just drifted into view.

"Hello, dear," said Mrs Cholsey. "We thought we might meet Timmy, didn't we, Lucy? We've just been up to the shops to get some fresh salad for your father's tea, and a few things for you to take camping. I hope we'll be back in time for Stacey and Karen. Did you have a nice day at school? Here, let me have your bag, dear. Have they given you a lot of homework? It's heavy today."

"Maths and geography," said Timothy. He walked on towards home with his mother.

"Mash and porridge!" shouted Marcus.

"Hush, Marcus," said Mrs Cholsey. "It's high time that child was at school. He's one of those that gets boisterous if he isn't given enough to do. Thank goodness you weren't like that, Timothy. His mother's at her wit's end, and it's another year before he goes to school. Now, Marcus, come away from there! Why don't you hold on to the buggy like Alvin? Alvin's always a good boy, aren't you?"

Alvin was holding the buggy on one side, and

twisting his bit of blanket and sucking two fingers on his other hand. Timothy supposed that he had been more like Alvin when he was small. It was strange to think of Alvin having ideas in his small head.

Turning into the next street they saw Karen and Stacey waiting at the front door.

"My Stacey!" Alvin shouted. He let go of the buggy to run towards her and tripped over the edge of a paving stone. Stacey ran to pick him up.

Just before they reached the front door, it opened. Mr Cholsey had been watching for them to come home. Timothy thought it was mean of him not to have let Karen and Stacey in because he must have seen them too if he was looking out of the hall window. He usually tried to pretend that the children Mrs Cholsey minded did not exist.

"That's my plans for the weekend down the drain," he shouted at Mrs Cholsey. "Thanks to you."

Mrs Cholsey put the brake on the buggy and began to unstrap the little children.

"Whatever do you mean, dear?" she asked. "We have just been buying some tins for your camping trip. Beans and corned beef. You know you like those."

Mr Cholsey stamped into the front room and turned the television on loud. Timothy hoped that the camping plans had gone right down the drain and not just been changed a little. He wondered what his mother could have done. She did not seem to know at all. She did not seem very worried either. She just carried on as usual, until Mr Cholsey should be ready to explain what was wrong. She even changed channels on the television so that the little children could watch a cartoon. Timothy wished he was as good at ignoring his father when he was angry.

When the little children were munching biscuits in front of the television and Karen and Stacey had taken theirs out to the tent, Mr Cholsey went into the kitchen. Timothy stayed to listen.

"So whose idea was it," said his father, "to put Timothy down on the standby list for his tonsils?"

Timothy's heart sank when he heard his name. He had had a feeling that the whole trouble might be somehow his fault. But when he heard the word 'tonsils' he felt easier, because even his father generally seemed to agree that he was not to blame for his troublesome tonsils, and sometimes sounded almost sympathetic.

"Whatever do you mean?" asked Mrs Cholsey, warming the teapot. "You know he has been on the waiting list for the operation since he was eight. Or was it when he was nine? I know it was just after we came back from Devon that he was really bad."

"I know that," said Mr Cholsey impatiently. "I know he was on the ordinary waiting list. But the hospital rang while you were out, and I heard all about that card you signed."

"Card?" said Mrs Cholsey vaguely. "Could you get those cups down, dear?"

Mr Cholsey ignored her and she had to stretch past

him to get the cups down from the shelf.

"You signed a card saying that Timothy could go in at short notice if anyone else dropped off the waiting list."

"Well, of course I did," said Mrs Cholsey. "It would mean he could have his tonsils done sooner if someone did drop out, wouldn't it?"

"Well, someone has," said Mr Cholsey. "And it happens to be this weekend. So your bright idea has wrecked my camping expedition."

Timothy was not sure whether this was good or bad news. He had been hoping so desperately for the camping trip to be called off that he had thought he would welcome anything that stopped it. But although he had known he was on the waiting list to have his tonsils taken out, he was not sure that he could really feel glad about it.

"Well, dear, I couldn't have known it would be this weekend," said Mrs Cholsey. "Could I? Besides, they surely don't do operations at the weekend, do they?"

"It's first thing Monday morning," said Mr Cholsey grimly, taking the first cup of tea that was poured out. "They want him in at midday on Sunday. So, are you going to ring them and cancel it?"

"Oh, I couldn't do that," said Mrs Cholsey, reaching over and stirring in Mr Cholsey's sugar for him. "I expect he would go right down to the bottom of the list again. Why don't you set off on Friday evening, and come back on Sunday morning? You could still have most of the weekend."

Timothy held his breath. He did not think he could bear to face a weekend of camping and hospital, one after the other. He waited to see whether his father would agree to this plan. There did not seem to be anything wrong with it.

"No, it's all right," said Mr Cholsey, with his chin in the air. "We just won't go. It's your decision. I would have thought the fresh air and exercise would have done the boy more good, but if that's how you feel, we'll forget it."

Timothy breathed again. He ran out into the garden and dived into the tent.

"I haven't got to go!" he shouted. "The camping's off!"

Stacey and Karen stared at him.

"I've never seen you look so excited about anything," said Karen. "I would have been furious if my dad had called off a camping trip. You are an odd person."

"Why can't you go?" asked Stacey. "Is that what your dad was so angry about?"

"I've got to go into hospital and have my tonsils out," said Timothy. "Someone else has cancelled their operation, so I'm going in their place."

"I hope it was someone having the same operation," said Karen, with a gleam in her eye. "Not someone having their leg off or something."

Timothy knew this was nonsense, but he felt a little uneasy.

"Don't take any notice," said Stacey. "She's only

teasing. You'll be in the Ears and Noses and Throats place, where I had my adenoids out. They don't do legs there. And they check about a hundred times that you are the right person for the operation. You'll have name tags all over you and the notes about you go with you everywhere."

"I've got to go in on Sunday at dinner-time," Timothy told them. "The operation is on Monday morning. Normally I would be dreading it, but it can't be worse than camping."

"Perhaps we'll come and visit you," said Stacey. "Karen's coming over to my flat on Sunday and staying the night, aren't you, Karen? Find out what the visiting times are, Timothy."

Timothy looked at Karen, who seemed quite happy at the idea of visiting him. He decided that nothing would be nicer than lying in hospital, where his father could not expect him to do anything, and being visited by Karen and Stacey. Then he would know that they thought of him as their friend.

"Knock knock!" someone shouted through the tent flap. "Can I come in?" Marcus crawled in and climbed on to Timothy's lap. He was still wearing the nasty little hat, but Timothy put his arms round him and said, "I'll take you into hospital with me instead of a teddy bear."

There were seven beds in the children's ward, and next to Timothy's was a big metal cot. The baby in it was standing up watching Timothy. It had a dummy in its mouth and it was dribbling. In the bed opposite, a boy was sleeping. Two girls were playing on the floor. The rest of the beds were empty.

Mr Cholsey unhooked the clipboard from the foot of Timothy's bed and flipped through the sheets of paper.

"There's a chart here for his pulse and temperature," he said. "And a sheet to fill in allergies, food preferences ... Toilet habits! I thought they would have put him in an adult ward instead of in with these babies."

"Well, he's used to little ones," said Mrs Cholsey. "He'll feel at home here." She unpacked Timothy's case into the locker by the bed. "But it is a bit crowded, isn't it? There's hardly room to get a chair between these beds. I don't know how the nurses manage. I'll put Minky Monkey on top of the locker with the squash bottle."

"Height, weight, blood group ... " read Mr Cholsey. Timothy wished his parents would go home.

A nurse came and took the clipboard from Mr Cholsey. She read the name on the top.

"Hello, Timothy," she said. "All settled in? I'm going to take your temperature now." She popped the thermometer into Timothy's mouth.

"Do you want him in his pyjamas?" asked Mrs Cholsey.

"You can keep your ordinary clothes on for now, if you like," the nurse said to Timothy. "Keep your pyjamas for bedtime. Then in the morning we'll be putting you into a hospital nightie for the operation. Won't that be lovely?" She grinned at Timothy. It was difficult for him to smile back with the thermometer in his mouth.

Two children came shyly into the room with their parents and the nurse went to show them their beds. Mr Cholsey stood up.

"Time we were off," he said.

"We'll be back to see you this evening, Timmy," said Mrs Cholsey. "Have you thought of anything you would like us to bring in for you? You've got enough books to read, haven't you? And there are lots of nice comics and games here."

Timothy looked round. There was a shelf running all the way round the room above the heads of the beds. It was crammed with books and toys, but they looked shabby and most of them were for much younger children.

"I'll do a puzzle," he mumbled, trying not to let cool air into his mouth.

Mrs Cholsey picked a puzzle with a picture of two boys fishing and put it on Timothy's bedtable.

"All right, then, dear?" she asked. "Shall I open your sweets for you?"

At last they left. Timothy put the puzzle back on the shelf and lay on the bed feeling happy. The rest of the day was his to do as he liked. Tomorrow he might be feeling too drowsy after the operation to enjoy himself, but today he could draw or eat or just lie and think.

The nurse came to look at the thermometer. She checked the paper bracelet on his wrist, which had his name and number on it, and drew a dot on Timothy's chart. Then she felt his pulse.

"There's nothing wrong with me yet," said Timothy.

"I know," said the nurse, taking the baby out of the cot and giving it a cuddle. "But I have to keep doing it all the same. Every two hours. After the operation it will be every half hour until we are sure you are back to normal. You are just in for tonsils, aren't you? You had better eat plenty today, then, because your throat will be too sore tomorrow for much eating, and after tea-time tonight you're not allowed anything to eat or drink."

"What's wrong with the baby?" asked Timothy.

Timothy 135

"This is Gemma," said the nurse. "The doctor's going to have a look at her ears. You're a sweetie-pie, aren't you, Gemma? She's ever so good, aren't you, gorgeous?"

The other boy woke up and called out, so the nurse put Gemma back in the cot and went to see to him. Gemma's mouth turned down at the corners and she drew in a long jerking breath ready to start sobbing. Timothy looked round for something to distract her. His toy monkey from home was on the locker and he gave that to her. She tucked it under her arm but still looked as though she might cry. He grabbed his drawing pad and pen and quickly drew a baby in a cot. Gemma watched.

"That's you," Timothy told her. "Look, you are happy, not sad. Now we'll draw the nurse. She's in such a rush she's put roller skates on so she can get around quicker."

He turned over the page. "Now I'll draw my new invention. Hospital bunk beds. That way they can fit in twice as many patients and cut down the waiting lists. In fact we'll have three beds on top of each other to save more space. Now the nurses have to have stilts to reach the patients at the top." Gemma stared at the page with round eyes. "Now this surgeon has had a transplant. He's got six arms now so that he can operate on three patients at once."

"Daddy!" shouted Gemma happily.

"Does that look like your daddy?" said Timothy doubtfully. He put a stethoscope round the doctor's neck and fixed a periscope to his cap. "Now he can inspect the patients on the top layer without getting up on his stilts." Timothy did not dare to stop drawing in case Gemma began to cry again. He was still drawing when someone tapped him on his shoulder. He turned round. Karen and Stacey stood there looking rather shy, each carrying her school bag, plimsoll bag and a large carrier bag.

"Oh, I am glad you came!" said Timothy. "Just a minute. I can't stop drawing in case this baby starts crying. I think she is missing her father."

"Those are nice pictures," said Karen. "What's this one?" she asked Gemma, pointing to someone bandaged all over.

"Daddy!" said Gemma.

"You've drawn hundreds," said Stacey. "We thought you would be just lying in your bed eating biscuits."

Timothy was not quite pleased by that. He did not want to be thought of as that sort of person, even though it was just what he had been planning to do.

"My mother brought in loads of food," he said. "Do you want some?"

"We brought you some food," said Karen. "Maybe you don't really need it. My downstairs neighbour sent a load of her left-over fruit. But Stacey and I were going to ask you if we could keep some of it anyway."

"Of course you can," said Timothy, rather puzzled. "But my mother never brought any fruit, only sweet things and crisps, so it would be nice to have an apple or something."

"You can have it all if you want," said Stacey. "Because it's really to be a present for you. But we need some food for a special reason."

"You've got an awful lot of luggage," said Timothy. "That's not all fruit, is it?"

Karen and Stacey looked at each other.

"Shall we tell him?" said Stacey. "It is his father's tent."

"All right," said Karen.

"My dad thinks I'm spending the night at Stacey's," said Karen.

"Well, you are, aren't you?" said Timothy. "You told me you were."

"And Karen asked my mum if I could go and stay with her instead," said Stacey. "It wasn't really a lie, because it was a question, and my mum said yes. So each of them thinks we are both staying with the other one."

Timothy was bewildered. "So where are you really staying?" he asked.

"In the tent!" said Karen. "We're camping out!"

"What – in my garden?" said Timothy. "My father never said you could, did he?"

"Of course he didn't," said Karen. "He's not going to know."

"How are you going to get into the garden?" asked Timothy. "Suppose they see you? They might think you were burglars!"

"We're not going through the house," Karen

explained. "We'll get into the garden along the edge of the river."

"I didn't know you could," said Timothy.

"That path at the end of your garden goes right along to the bridge," said Karen. Timothy guessed that she was the one who had hatched the plan. "We'll go there and wait until it's safe. Do your mum and dad draw those living room curtains in the evening?" She seemed to have thought of every detail.

"Yes," said Timothy. "After tea. Otherwise the sun shines on the television."

"Right," said Karen. "Once we see the curtains are drawn we'll sneak down the garden into the tent. They aren't likely to come out looking in the tent, are they?"

"No, I shouldn't think so," said Timothy. "My father isn't very interested in it any more. My mother asked him to leave it up for a while because the little ones like playing in it. But what will you sleep on? The grass will get wet with the dew, won't it? And it will be cold."

"I've got all my gran's plastic carrier bags. She hoards them, so I've got plenty to spread out under us. And when I told her I was playing camping she let me sew an old blanket up into a sleeping bag."

"I've just got an ordinary blanket," said Stacey. "I told Mum that Karen's dad was a bit short of blankets, and she let me borrow it. She wanted me to take a whole lot of pillowcases and things as well, but I told her Karen's gran might get a bit funny and think we were criticising her for not having enough sheets."

Timothy wished that he had had the idea first. It would have been quite easy for him to slip out into the garden once his parents were in bed, and if he had spent a night out in the tent, then perhaps Karen and Stacey would think him as adventurous as themselves. He wondered what it would be like in the garden in the middle of the night. The worst that could happen would be that one of the neighbours' cats would come prowling by.

"So you need the food for camping," he said. "You'd better take it all. They'll give me my tea here and I'm not allowed to eat after that anyway."

"We can't take it all," said Karen. "It's very heavy. Mrs Appleton gave us a melon and it weighs a ton. It's a bit squashy on one side. You'll need to cut that bit off."

They emptied the bags on to the bed. Gemma made hungry noises and reached out for the bananas. The nurse went past.

"Goodness, Timothy," she said. "You've got some good friends! I wouldn't mind some of that. You had better get a bowl from the kitchen to put it in."

"Can we give the baby a banana?" asked Stacey.

The nurse checked Gemma's notes. "Yes, that's all right. You hungry, Gemma?"

Stacey peeled a banana and passed it through the bars of the cot. Gemma put half of it in her mouth and tucked the other half under her arm with the monkey.

"That's a nice monkey," said Stacey. "Is it a hospital monkey?"

"It's mine from home," said Timothy. "I lent it to her. My mother packed it for me. She thought I would want to cuddle it. She calls it Minky Monkey."

"It has a lovely smile," said Stacey. "I've got a monkey but its face wore off. You might need it tomorrow when you are feeling awful after the operation. I had to borrow a horrible plastic clown when I was in for my adenoids and I did wish I had brought one of my old animals from home."

"Will I be feeling awful?" asked Timothy. "I thought they were supposed to be making me better."

"You might be lucky," said Stacey. "The girl next to me was fine. She had her operation just before me, and by the time I woke up she was running around and playing. I did feel bad. But it didn't last long."

They sorted out the fruit and packed some of Timothy's crisps and biscuits in with Karen's sleeping bag. Stacey had a thermos flask in her bag.

"They might bring me a cup of tea later," said Timothy. "You could have that."

"There's a hot drinks machine downstairs," said Stacey. "We have already put one cup of drinking chocolate in, but we thought we had better save the rest of our money in case of emergencies. I suppose tea would mix in all right. Ask for three sugars if they do bring you some."

Both the girls had their clean school clothes neatly

packed in their carriers, with toothbrushes, hair-brushes and anything else that their parents had thought they might need for the night away or for the next day at school.

The nurse came past again. She looked into Gemma's cot and closed her eyes. The banana was squashed all over the sheets.

"Oh, I'm sorry," said Stacey. "She was eating it and then I stopped watching. It might wipe off."

"Don't worry," said the nurse. "I was going to give her a bath straight after tea. I might as well do it now and change the sheets at the same time."

"Is Timothy allowed to walk about?" Stacey asked the nurse. "When I was here there was a little room with rocking horses and things in it. I thought we could go and have a look."

"Oh, he can walk about," said the nurse. "He's not an invalid. But they have moved all the big toys down to the new children's ward. Go right down to the end of the corridor, turn left, and through the double doors. You can't miss it. Don't be too long, because they will be round with the drinks soon."

The new children's ward was huge and bright. It had yellow walls and curtains with pictures on. The beds had coloured covers and there was plenty of space. There were easels for painting, a Wendy house, two rocking horses, a giant dolls' house and a big wooden engine that several small children could ride on. There were little basins next to the big ones, and in one corner there were comfortable armchairs arranged in a ring. But there were no children in the ward. In fact there was no-one there at all.

Karen and Stacey jumped up on the rocking horses and began to gallop. Timothy knelt down and peeped through the windows into the dolls' house.

"It opens," said Karen. "I can see the catch from here."

"I like them shut," said Timothy. "I like looking in from outside. It looks more real."

He opened the house, rearranged the things inside, and then shut the front again. While he was peeping through the windows some people came into the ward. One was in a white coat, one in a suit and the other was a young woman with green hair, wearing orange trousers and a rainbow-coloured shirt.

"This is the new children's ENT ward," said the woman in the white coat, who was a doctor. "It was finished last summer, but we haven't the staff to open it."

"Where are all the children, then?" asked the man in the suit.

"We have eight children's beds in an old four-bed ward down at the other end," said the doctor. "It's not enough. There are long waiting lists. I think these beds are used for parents who are staying in overnight with their children, but apart from that the whole ward is wasted. It's criminal."

"It's lovely," said the green-haired person. "So bright. Children would love it. Is the other ward like this?"

"No," said the doctor. "It's pretty grim. But come and see for yourself. And have a look at this corridor that we were thinking about." She led the way out of the ward. The man in the suit followed her, but the green-haired woman stayed behind. She came over to where Karen and Stacey were still galloping.

"Hello," she said. "Are you visiting someone here?"

"Yes," said Karen and Stacey.

"No," said Timothy.

"This is one of the patients," said Karen. "They are going to cut bits off him tomorrow."

"Only small bits," said Timothy. "My tonsils."

"We came down here to play," said Stacey. "There isn't room for big toys like this in the real children's ward."

"It's a shame they can't use this ward," said the woman. She wandered out.

"We ought to go back," said Karen. "Timothy will miss his cup of tea and we need it for the flask."

They had a last ride on the horses and set off back to the children's ward.

There was a trolley in the middle of the ward, and a man in a blue overall was pouring out drinks.

"Squash or tea?" he called to Timothy.

"Tea, please," said Timothy. "Does this count as tea-time? Is this the last thing I'll be allowed?"

"No," said the man. "That will be proper tea-time, with food." He poured out a cup for Timothy and was surprised how quickly Timothy handed him back the empty cup.

"You were thirsty," he said. "I can't give you another. This is only the beginning of my round and I don't want to run out before I get down to the men's ward."

The three people that they had seen in the bright new children's ward were over by Timothy's bed. When Timothy had finished with the tea, he noticed that they were looking at his drawing book. Gemma was looking very clean with fluffy dried hair and a new pink nightie. She was leaning her chin on the rail of the cot and watching them turn the pages of the drawings that Timothy had made for her.

"These are great," said the woman with green hair. "Are you Timothy Cholsey?" she asked. "Did you draw them?"

"Yes," said Timothy. "I just did them quickly because that baby was crying and I was trying to amuse her. They are not very careful."

"No, no, they are really lovely," said the doctor. "What do you think?" she asked the man in the suit.

The man turned to Timothy. "We had better explain," he said. "The hospital is keen to brighten up this part of the hospital, especially as it looks like being some time before the new children's ward can be opened. My organisation has raised a little money for a redecoration project, and Martha here is an art student who has kindly volunteered to design a mural for the corridor. We were wondering what sort of design would appeal to children when we saw your lovely pictures."

"I thought we could base part of the design on your drawings," said Martha. "Do you have any other ideas? I thought we could have one wall with humorous hospital scenes, and the other section with something quite different, to take people's minds off hospital."

"Mountains and castles," said Stacey.

"A fun-fair," said Karen. "Fantastic, Timothy! Think of me being friends with a real artist! And everyone who comes here will see your pictures on the wall."

"It's only a suggestion at this stage," said the man in the suit. "The drawings may need to be adapted to fit the walls in the corridors. And of course you can't tell what the hospital administrators are going to approve. But it's a splendid idea."

"It will be terrific," said Martha. "I'm sure they will agree to it."

Timothy took back the drawing book. "I'll think about it," he said. "How would you make the pictures big enough for the wall?"

"That's easy," said Stacey. "We did it at school with maps. You need to draw a grid all over, so that the whole picture is divided into squares. Then you mark up squares on the wall, only much bigger, and that makes it easy to copy. Whatever is in the first little square, you copy on to the first big square on the wall, and so on. That way you keep it in proportion."

"When are you going to paint it?" asked Karen.

"As soon as I can," said Martha. "I can't wait."

"Well," said the man in the suit. "The money's there. You only have to buy the paint, Martha."

"We have to get clearance for the designs," said the doctor. "But I don't think that should be a problem. It just depends how soon they can be ready."

"I'll do what I can this evening," said Timothy. "But if I don't finish them, I can't promise anything for tomorrow. I may not be feeling up to it after the operation."

"I'll call in tomorrow evening," said Martha, "and see how you have got on. But there is no rush. We can arrange to meet when you are out of hospital. You've got quite a talent, haven't you? Don't worry if you think you haven't got enough ideas. Once we get together and start working out the shapes of the walls we've got to cover, the ideas will soon come."

"I must get back to work," said the doctor.

"I should be going, too," said the man in the suit. "Thanks for showing us your pictures, Timothy." Although he had really looked at them without being shown.

"We couldn't help with the painting, could we?" Stacey asked Martha as she was leaving.

Martha looked at her. "It's an important job," she said. "You would have to be very neat. But it would be nice to have some help."

"Oh, yes," said Karen. "We'll help. If we aren't neat enough, we can help mix the colours or paint the big patches like sky and grass. I would love to. Can we?"

"Timothy can tell me tomorrow how to contact you," said Martha. "I'll let you know when the painting is going to start. Good luck with your tonsils, Timothy."

"Let's go," said Stacey when Martha had left. "There won't be many buses on a Sunday evening. I don't want to be out late at night."

"You are going to be out all night," said Timothy.

"Yes," agreed Stacey. "But in a nice cosy tent, not hanging around at bus-stops. Come on, Karen. Thanks for the tea, Timothy."

"Good luck," said Timothy. "Thanks for visiting me. It was really nice to see you."

They set off with their bags while Timothy picked up his pen and began to fill a few more pages of the drawing book.

Timothy | **CHAPTER SIX**

After Stacey and Karen had left for their night in the tent, the man in blue brought the food round. There was cheese on toast and ice cream. Timothy used his knife to cut up the squashy melon and ate three slices of it before the nurse came to hang a sign saying 'Nil by mouth' above his bed.

"I'll put your fruit and biscuits up on the shelf," she said. "So you're not tempted. And it means nothing to drink either. I'll be going off in a little while, and the night shift will be taking over. I'd better get Gemma settled down for the night." She went to warm up milk for Gemma's bedtime bottle.

It was quite late when Mr and Mrs Cholsey arrived with another bag of biscuits and crisps. They looked very smart. Mrs Cholsey had make-up on and Mr Cholsey was wearing his best tie.

"I'm not allowed to eat anything," said Timothy. "But I'll keep it for tomorrow. You'd better put it all out of reach in case I'm hungry in the night."

"We won't stop for long, dear," said Mrs Cholsey.

"We're going out for the evening."

Timothy thought his parents should be sitting at home worrying about him, instead of rushing out to enjoy themselves as soon as he was out of the way. They tried to chat for a little, but he could see that they were in a hurry to be off.

"They say the weather's going to break tonight," Mr Cholsey said. "Heavy rain expected. Do you know this month has had the highest average temperatures for eighteen years?"

"Really, dear?" said Mrs Cholsey. "I thought it was very warm. Eighteen years! Goodness me." She looked at her finger nails, which were shiny pink this evening.

Timothy thought of Stacey and Karen sleeping in the tent and wondered what it would be like with rain battering down on the canvas. He hoped it would not thunder.

"We should have taken that tent down," said Mrs Cholsey. "We don't want it getting drenched."

"I'll do it this evening," said Mr Cholsey. "When we get home. I should have put it away last week, but you would insist on me leaving it up."

"There are some nice programmes on the television tonight," Mrs Cholsey told Timothy. "I expect there's a television here."

"Yes," said Timothy. He was trying to think of a way of warning Karen and Stacey that his father was planning to take the tent down that evening. He did not dare to imagine what his father would say when he found them inside. And how would they feel if he just unhooked the guy-ropes without looking inside, and the tent collapsed on top of them?

"I'll be fine," he said. "Have a nice evening. I'll see you tomorrow, Mummy."

Mrs Cholsey gave him a kiss on the cheek and his father patted him on the shoulder.

"Don't worry, son," he said. "They used to do tonsils without an anaesthetic when I was a boy. Nothing to it."

They left and Timothy sprang off the bed. He wished he had not put his pyjamas on just before his parents arrived. He looked round the ward. Gemma and the smaller children were asleep. A mother was reading aloud to the two girls at the other end of the ward. The nurse seemed to have left.

Timothy grabbed his shoes and clothes from the locker by his bed and squashed them into a little bundle. Then he took his towel and wrapped it round them. He could see no way to warn Stacey and Karen except to go home himself and tell them what his father planned to do. He could walk down the corridor with his towel bundle and look as though he was just going for a bath. But what would the nurses say when they saw that his bed was still empty later on?

Then Timothy remembered that the nurses were changing shifts. The night nurses had not even seen him yet. If he made his bed look unused, they might not notice that he was missing at all. He straightened the sheets, which was easy because he had only sat on top of them, not got underneath. Then he cleared his drawing pad and books away into the locker and took the used sheets off the clip-board at the foot of the bed and put them carefully in the locker. The bed looked just as it had when he arrived.

He decided not to leave straight away for fear of bumping into his parents leaving the hospital. They had probably come by car and would go straight to the car park, but they might be travelling by bus or walking straight into town. He would hide in the bathroom for a while. When his parents had had time to get away from the hospital he would slip out in his clothes and nobody would know that he was an escaped patient and not just a late visitor leaving a friend.

Getting home might be a problem. He was not sure which was the right bus stop for home, because there was a one-way system around the hospital and all the buses stopped on the same side of the road. He thought there must be signs saying which stop was which, but as he did not often travel by bus he did not feel very confident about it. He might have to ask someone. He hoped he had enough change in his jacket pocket for the fare. He would check when he was safely in the bathroom. The first thing was to get safely out of the ward without being noti͏ hoped the mother was worried enou͏ remem- little girl not to bother abou͏ hidden in the

On the way to t͏ bered that t͏ Timothy 153

garden shed at home, so if the worst came to the worst, and he could not find the right bus-stop or he had not enough money, he could take a taxi and then go indoors and fetch money to pay for it when they reached the house. He wondered whether a taxi would stop for a child. Perhaps the driver would just think he was playing.

He did not bother to think what the nurses would say when he arrived back to move into his empty bed, with the chart not filled in for the hours he had been missing. There would be time enough to worry about that on the journey home. He hoped they would not refuse to do the operation because they couldn't be sure that he had not been out eating and drinking while they had not been watching. He hoped that he could sneak back in without even being noticed, put the sheets back on the clipboard with some invented dots for his pulse and temperature, and the tired night nurse would just say, "Goodness! I could have sworn this bed was empty earlier! How absent-minded I must be getting!"

The bathroom door was locked, and so was the other one further up the corridor. Timothy headed for the toilets, but he could hear a nurse talking to someone in there. In a panic, he raced along the ~~rridor. Perhaps there would be more bathrooms to dressmen's wards further along. But when he came They w~ bathroom, he noticed two men in

seemed to be watching him. a child was going into the

adults' bathroom in pyjamas and coming out again in his clothes. They might mention it to a nurse.

The whole thing seemed so complicated and difficult that he longed to go straight back to bed and fall asleep to forget it all, but he could not let Stacey and Karen be discovered in the tent by his father.

Suddenly he remembered the new children's ward. The doctor had said that parents sometimes slept there while their children were in hospital, but most likely they would still be with their children at this time of the evening, or in the canteen or the television room. He could get dressed there and hide his towel. It was quite reasonable for him to be going down there to look at the toys, so he felt more relaxed as he sauntered down the corridor.

Nobody was in the ward and the lights were off. The sun had gone down but it was not dark yet. Timothy walked softly down to the far end where two of the beds were partitioned off from the rest of the ward, and quickly began to dress. He left his pyjama jacket on under his jumper, but looking in the mirror he saw that the crumpled stripy collar was unmistakable, and he decided to put a shirt on instead. He was just tying his shoe laces when he heard footsteps. They were in the ward and coming closer. He held his breath. He hoped the person would not come as far as this. It would have been all right to have been caught coming along the corridor to play with the toys, but he did not know how he could explain being almost fully dressed in an unused ward.

The footsteps stopped and he heard a whispered voice. There must be two people. He heard a scraping, jingling sound and guessed that the curtains had been pulled closed round one of the beds. They hung on metal hooks on a rail on the ceiling and would probably make that kind of sound. Perhaps some parents had been up late last night with a sick child and were now going early to bed. Timothy decided to wait until he could be sure they were asleep, and then tiptoe out. He finished tying his laces, hid his pyjamas and towel in a bed-side locker and waited.

The people did not sound very sleepy. They were very quiet, but the sounds that Timothy could make out were surprising. There were giggles and squeaks. Timothy decided that it must be children. He was surprised that the hospital allowed sisters and brothers to stay in the empty ward, but at least he had little to fear from children. He set off down the ward.

He was half-way to the door when a very loud whisper made him freeze.

"Timothy! What are you doing?"

He swung round, and saw Karen and Stacey peeping out from inside the closed curtain. He ran back to them and went inside the curtain.

"I thought you would have set off by now!" he said. "You mustn't go! My father thinks it is going to rain, and he is going to take the tent down tonight. It won't be safe for you to sleep there. Oh, I am glad to see you."

"We already had set off," said Stacey. "But we got

on the wrong bus. It was the right number, but it was going the wrong way. Karen just asked for 'the last stop before the High Street', and there must be another High Street at the other end of the bus route. That used up nearly all our money, so we couldn't afford to get on another bus going the right way. So we decided to come back and spend the night here. You'll have to get your father to put the tent up again when it stops raining because we're going to do it next weekend instead."

"I wish we could have spent the night out in the rain," said Karen. "It would be so nice to be all warm and cosy in the tent with the storm just the other side of the canvas. But what are you doing here, Timothy? Were you playing with the toys? Why were you tiptoeing about like that?"

"I was coming to warn you!" said Timothy. "I told you, my father is going to take the tent down tonight, so I was going to come on the bus and tell you not to camp there. I hadn't thought about where you could spend the night. I had to come in here to get dressed. I was in my pyjamas when my mother and father came to see me."

"But did the nurses let you go?" asked Karen. "I thought they were taking your pulse and everything, and looking after you."

"I sneaked out before the night nurses came on duty," said Timothy. "I made my bed look as though no-one had used it. So I hope they won't notice that anyone is missing. I suppose I had better get back quickly before they notice that there isn't anyone to be missing. I can go back like this, because they don't know that I had already changed into my pyjamas. Hey, you will need money for the bus in the morning." He felt in his jacket pocket. "Here's a pound. Sleep well. And don't giggle so much. Anybody could hear you."

He hurried back to his own ward. Two nurses were looking at the clipboard on his bed.

"Are you Timothy Cholsey?" one of them asked. "We've been looking for you. Do you know what has happened to your chart and your notes? We can't find them anywhere."

"Oh, I think my father was looking at them," said Timothy. "I expect he left them in the locker."

The nurse took them out. "They must always be on the end of the bed," she said. "You tell your dad. Have you been for a wash? Good boy. You had better get into your pyjamas now. Look, the others are all asleep. You want a good rest before your operation."

Timothy was the first to be taken down to the operating theatre in the morning. He was wheeled on a trolley by two men in green coats and white boots.

"Don't be frightened," they said, as they pushed the trolley towards the lifts. "It'll all be over before you know it."

Timothy smiled cheerfully up at them. The doors of one of the lifts were sliding shut. Timothy looked round, and just had time to see Karen, waving at him, and Stacey, trying not to be noticed in a corner. So nobody had discovered them in their hospital beds and now they must be setting off for school. They vanished as the doors met, and the lights above the lift showed that they had reached the ground floor. Timothy imagined them leaving the hospital. Karen would be strolling, Stacey trying to hurry her along, to get safely outside.

Under the anaesthetic Timothy had long happy dreams about the pictures that he and Stacey and Karen were going to paint along all the corridors in the hospital and all the way along the bus route home. And he did not feel too bad when he woke up.

A FEW FAIR DAYS
Jane Gardam

Enter the weird and wonderful world of Lucy's childhood. Meet Aunt Fanny, Auntie Bea and Aunt Kitty (who never stop travelling). Discover for yourself Jinnie Love's Fair Days, nanny-nuns, akkerbeests, polycarps and queeds. Marvel over the stories of Mr Crossley's wig, the great ship, the magus Zoroaster and the beast in the mire... But above all, prepare to be thoroughly entertained!

"Jane Gardam writes beautifully both for children and adults... An enchanting book." *The Lady*

"A modern classic... It's a very evocative book." *BBC Radio*